CONTENTS

THE HEIRESS'S SECRET LOVE

The Balfour Hotel Book 1

AMANDA DAVIS

A forced betrothal, a missing chambermaid, and two unlikely allies whose lives merge in a forbidden entanglement of the heart.

Emmaline is to be married to a heartless brute of a man—sold off like a pig at auction, nothing more than a pawn to secure her father's business dealings.

When the handsome Elias Compton arrives at the hotel under the guise of seeking employment, she is instantly smitten.

Elias has come to The Balfour Hotel undercover. His real mission is to search for a missing woman who was last seen working as a chambermaid at the hotel.

Has she met with foul play?

Does the fiancé of the beautiful Emmaline Balfour have anything to do with her disappearance?

One thing is for certain. There are some sinister goings on at the hotel

As Emmaline and Elias join forces to find the whereabouts of the missing chambermaid, they soon become entangled in affairs of the heart.

PROLOGUE

Sweeping winds flowed from either side of the Thames, leaving Christiana cold and wary as she peered about. There was a foreboding in the air, one which she could not easily identify but which fell heavily over her thinly cloaked shoulders. She wished she had thought to dress more warmly but she had not expected to be out for so long.

What has become of him? She wondered, looking about the banks of the river before rubbing her worn mittens to create a small friction through the wool. It was high time she knit new ones. The winter cold seeped into her bones like clever little knives, knowing precisely which entry to seek.

If all goes well enough, I will have someone else to knit me mittens, she thought. *Perhaps I will have an abigail to knit my outer clothes and another for my articles.*

It was likely the reason she had not done so herself already; Christiana was clinging to the hope that her future would be much brighter than her present appeared in those moments.

Somewhere in the distance, she heard the ringing of church bells, indicating that the hour of six had arrived, yet she remained in wait.

Has he not taken me seriously? She wondered, a fusion of panic and ire sparking within, the emotions warming away the chill of the eve. *I hope he is not so bold as to leave me here, not when so much is at risk.*

There was no way for her to know, not when she had stood at the location for over an hour.

I must return to the hotel, she thought, gathering her cloak and spinning downwind. It was a relief to remove the sting from her face, and idly she wondered why she had not done so sooner, but Christiana had never been known for her wits. With stinging eyes, she blinked away tears and made her way toward the street holding her skirts firmly within her grip as she moved.

The rain began then, an icy pelt which began to pound upon her without mercy and Christiana slipped against the slick rocks as she attempted her climb upward.

My word, she thought furiously, fighting to regain her footing. *What else could go awry?*

It was the wrong question to ask the heavens for as the words passed through her mind, a clap of thunder caused her to startle and gasp for air. She paused a moment, only to catch her breath, and looked behind her once more. The wind assaulted her face. Her cheeks stung as her cerulean eyes took notice of a form drawing near.

Pivoting fully, her heart in her throat, she raised a gloved hand to wave but through the now-driving rain, she was suddenly unsure if the figure approaching was the one she had been waiting upon.

She opened her mouth to call out but the name was lost against another rumble of thunder. A flash of lightning illuminated the winter sky, creating a streak of white light upon the newcomer's face yet she could barely make it out.

Christiana froze, her jaw slack with fear as her bowels seemed to turn to water.

It is not him, she realized. Yet the man stalked closer, his hat pulled down to shield his face as though he did not wish to be detected. There was no godly reason for any soul to be down by the river banks at that hour on a winter's night, not for good cause. It was why Christiana had chosen it, after all.

Nothing good can come of me being here, she thought desperately, whirling back to climb over the rocks again. She did not give herself time nor grace as she scrambled to climb to the top of the bank but she quickly realized that her movements were to no avail. She continued sliding back down the sleek sides of the wide boulders.

Fear threatened to swallow her whole but Christiana knew she must not be caught by the man who drew closer with every slip she made.

He sent this one here, Christiana thought mournfully. *I should never have put him in such a position. How much did he pay this one? Is it enough?*

It was unfathomable to believe, but as she fell for the final time, her drenched clothes collapsing around her, Christiana began to sob.

The man was at her side now, the brim of his top hat still shadowing his face but Christiana knew precisely who he was and why he had come.

"Please!" she moaned, holding her hands up as if to ward the inevitable away. "Please, no matter how much he paid you to do this, it is not enough. Think about our history together!"

"Good evening, Christiana," he said pleasantly but the gleam in his eye contradicted his genial tone and there was little doubt what he had come to do. Slowly, she looked to him, his even voice unnerving her more than his presence and the mounting storm combined.

"Why?" she cried. "Why would he do this?"

He shrugged in the most casual way.

"You are becoming a nuisance, Christiana. You cannot fault him for wishing to see the end of this."

She closed her eyes again and hung her head, knowing that she was helpless.

"Do whatever you must," she sighed with resignation although her heart continued to pound with intense ferocity.

"This is not my decision to make, you understand," he told her quietly. "It stands solely with you."

The words confused Christiana more deeply than she was already and she stared at him imploringly, her blue eyes wide.

"I-I do not understand," she murmured. "What is your intention, then?"

He sighed heavily and reached for her hand to help her to her feet but Christiana did not accept his assistance even though the rain crept down the folds of her cloak and slithered against her frozen skin.

"If you come with me, your fate will be revealed," he told her, refusing to withdraw his hand. "You need not make this more difficult than it already is, Christiana. Please, do as I say."

She maintained her crouched position, lowering her head like she hoped he would simply disappear but she was not so naïve to believe in such a miracle.

"Christiana." His tone was no longer amiable. "You will come with me, one way or another."

From deep within her, she felt a yearning for survival creep to the surface waiting to erupt. She lifted her head and stared at him defiantly, their eyes clashing in the darkness. Foolishly, he seemed to think he had won and a slow smile formed on his lips.

"Come along now," he insisted, looking about for the first time, apparently concerned that they might be seen. "We have not much time."

Christiana shook her sopping head of dark hair.

"I will go nowhere with you," she hissed. "Do what you must but I refuse to make this easy for you!"

Without warning, she threw her head back and released a scream to match the howling wind swirling about them and watched as his face turned black with anger.

"As you wish," he countered, he raised his hand as if to strike her and suddenly Christiana's world went black.

CHAPTER ONE

It was the usual bustle of early morning with one extra charge to the already busy atmosphere; a slew of potential chambermaids and bell-boys flocked to the service entrance to be gauged for competency.

A rush of subdued but excited chatter filled Emmeline's ears as she wandered through the vast kitchen. Her golden-green eyes studied the influx of bodies impassively but inside, she shared in their budding anticipation.

The winter brought much strife with it to Luton and a need to staff the prestigious Balfour Hotel to capacity. With the cold came the need to keep the fireplaces lit, the blankets washed and the guests required more to remain in comfort than during the summer months.

It was one of Emmeline's favorite times of the year, the eager, fresh faces determined to make a good impression as they stood as polished and poised as could be given their limited means. They traveled from all across the country simply for an interview in the prestigious hotel but if they were hired, it was well worth the trials.

The Balfour Hotel was known across England as a fair employer, feeding and lodging their employees while paying them a decent wage. Their policies were unheard of in such a climate and yet it had always been as such.

It is also why we are presented with the best servants by the flock.

"Miss Balfour, may I fetch something for you?" Antoinette asked, her brow furrowing. Emmeline's presence seemed to daunt her on such a hectic morning.

"No, madam. I have simply come to examine the new prospects," Emmeline replied sweetly, turning her eyes toward the harried house-keeper. "You need not mind me."

Antoinette managed a smile but Emmeline could see that she would much prefer if the proprietor's daughter stayed clear away from the hiring process. It mattered little to Emmeline, however. It was a near tradition for her after all her years at the hotel. For as long as she could recall, she had risen early on the mornings of the hire to dress with special care and greet the newcomers.

It was a difficult concept for anyone else in the hotel to accept but Emmeline had always regarded the servants as more than merely employees, despite her parents' constant disapproval.

"They are not your equals, Emmy," her father, Charlton, often told her. "They are here to serve the hotel and the Balfours."

Emmeline would always nod agreeably, knowing that arguing with a man like Charlton Balfour was an exercise in futility. In her heart, however, the staff was much more than that to her.

After all, she had been raised among them and their children since the time of her birth, one and twenty years earlier.

Although Xavier was her blood brother, the children of the servants had become just as much her siblings as if they had been borne of the same parents. Even Xavier who had also run amok with the servant's children, was not as endeared to the servants as she found herself to be.

"Miss Balfour, may I assist you in some way?"

The maître d' stood before her and Emmeline realized she had lost herself in thought as bodies continued to flow about her in a sea of skirts and waistcoats, each one perfectly groomed with clean hands and nails and well-brushed hair. It made Emmeline proud to gaze upon them.

"No, Honor. I am well, thank you," she told him. "Please, go about your business as though I am not here."

"Very well, Miss."

He bowed slightly, his shiny head of blonde hair reflecting in the freshly polished pots hanging above the stove. Honor was young for the position, a man of only three and thirty but he had inherited the title of waiter overseer from his father who had served the hotel for two generations.

And yet he still refers to me as "Miss Balfour."

There was no cause for Honor or Antoinette to speak to her formally and no matter how often Emmeline gently asked them to call her by her Christian name, they did not oblige her request. She knew they feared the repercussions of being caught far more than they longed to accommodate her.

Perhaps one day, she thought, sighing as she moved out of the way to watch as the staff lined to be examined.

Emmeline stood near the wood stove and, in her fine dress of white lace and blue that swept about her mutton boots, she was careful not to block the outpouring of heat. The rain had finally ended but the day was still very cold at such an hour, not that Emmeline expected it to warm much more than it had. The sun struggled to shine through the thickness of heavy grey clouds above.

She wrapped her wool shawl about her shoulders, her back to the cold wall and listened as the interview commenced.

"Name?" Antoinette demanded, looking to her roster as she marched down the line of hopeful chambermaids.

"Name?" Honor asked the same as he, too, strolled about the waiting male staff.

"Jackson Benson."

"Catherine Munch."

"Joseph Calvin."

"Veronica Summer."

On and on the list went until all dozen men and women were accounted for, their names ticked off the list.

Emmeline studied each face, memorizing the features of the people who she might come to know but her attention was distracted as the service door opened and a lone man hurried inside.

"Forgive me," he called, raising his hands as though he surrendered himself in battle. "My coach was terribly detained. Am I too late?"

The anxiety upon his face was clear and his aquamarine eyes danced from Honor to Antoinette and back again as he attempted to seek absolution for the sin of tardiness.

"You are too late," Antoinette snapped, turning away to address the maids again. "We do not tolerate tardiness at the Balfour Hotel. We serve royalty, gentlemen of status. You may see yourself out the same way you came and be discrete about it."

Emmeline's heart caught in her throat as she saw the look of panic in his eyes.

"Please!" he protested. "The fault was not mine. I left Peterborough last night and have traveled straight through. I beg of you, do not dismiss me form this opportunity before you have given me a chance to prove my worth!"

Antoinette spun to glare at him, her mouth parting to speak, but before she could utter a word, Honor interjected.

"I will handle this, Mrs. Baxter. What is your name, boy?"

Antoinette whirled around to gape at Honor, her face displaying without hindrance, the contempt she felt. Emmeline stifled a sigh.

It had not been an easy transition for the older housekeeper to accept her younger counterpart. Honor's father and Antoinette had had a bond for decades, one which she undoubtedly still longed for. Honor was much more progressive in his treatment of the staff, something which the housekeeper found distasteful.

"Elias Compton, sir." The young man shuffled forward, his hat in his hands. Through her peripheral vision, Emmeline noted Honor's brow furrow. His eyes narrowed before he glanced at his sheet and nodded slowly but Emmeline's attention was fixed mostly on the handsome man before them. He was not as young as she had initially thought, given his dramatic entrance.

Seven and twenty? Eight and twenty? She guessed silently.

His hair was a deep ebony, too long for a waiter, but kept neatly back in a tie. The structure of his face was fine boned, almost regal, and if Emmeline had seen him in another setting, she might have mistaken him for royalty.

THE HEIRESS'S SECRET LOVE

Albeit not with those worn shoes.

Her amber eyes moved along the threadbare clothing and along the broad chest back to his face. He wore a poor man's clothes, just as the other hopefuls, yet there was something about the way he spoke and presented himself which did not echo lowly breeding.

Abruptly, he, too, lifted his head and met Emmeline's curious gaze as if he could feel her eyes upon him. Heat rose on Emmeline's cheeks and she quickly looked away, her pulse quickening at being caught boldly gawking at the stranger.

"I see your name here, Mr. Compton. Tell us, why should I entertain the idea of granting you an interview when you have already displayed a propensity for tardiness?" Honor demanded. There was an edge to his voice which Emmeline had not heard before.

He is attempting to assert his authority, Emmeline reasoned.

"I implore you, Mr....?" Elias peered at Honor questioningly.

"You will answer my question firstly and perhaps then I will offer you my name," Honor replied with uncharacteristic sharpness. Emmeline cringed at his tone. She desperately wished to speak up on behalf of Mr. Compton, whomever he was, but she knew it was not her place.

They already wish I were not here, she reminded herself. *You need not interject yourself in the middle of proceedings which have nothing to do with you.*

"Sir, I am a man of great ethic both in employment and in my personal nature. I shall always put this hotel above my own needs and be at the service of the guests and the Balfour family whenever I am needed."

There was a plaintiveness about him, his eyes growing wider with each word he spoke and as he continued his monologue, Emmeline felt her gaze again fixing on his passionate face.

"I have traveled a great distance with the last pence in my pockets to be here when there are many other inns which would have had me given my vast experience as a waiter. I beg of you, do not turn me away or I will have nowhere to go. I will not disappoint you again. I swear it."

Emmeline heard a sigh and she looked about to see that she was not alone in her swooning. The chambermaids each stared at him with adoring eyes, the combination of his endearing demeanor and dashing looks too much to ignore.

If Emmeline did not know better, she might have guessed that Antoinette was also moved by his speech but any hint of warmth quickly vanished from the housekeeper's eyes when she noticed Emmeline's gaze upon her.

"We will not permit another mistake," Honor told him sternly and Emmeline's body sagged with relief as though her own position rested on the maître d's words.

"You will need not permit one," Elias assured him. "I will not make another mistake. I swear it."

"Step into line. The interview has not yet started," Honor ordered him but he did not lose the strange expression on his face.

The young man did as he was told and stepped beside a tall boy on the end, his shoulders squared as he waited for instructions. Antoinette turned her attention back to the women and Emmeline realized she was wringing her hands, her long fingers twirling over the string of pearls along her neck.

I should not be here, she thought suddenly, her body unnaturally warm. Discretely, she moved toward the doorway but not without casting one last glance over her shoulder at Elias Compton. To her utter shock, he was staring boldly, unblinkingly, at her.

He must learn to show more decorum if he wishes to succeed here, she thought, her breaths suddenly escaping in short rasps. She scurried out of the kitchen and up the short flight of stairs into the dining room which still hosted breakfast diners.

"Are you ill?" A voice in her ear asked and Emmeline squealed in shock. She spun to face her brother who was just as surprised by her reaction.

"My word, Xavier! You cannot sneak upon me like that!"

"Sneak upon you?" he echoed, laughing. "You looked precisely in my direction when you entered. I smiled at you and you returned my smile. Are you unwell? Your face is the color of fresh strawberries and you are acting beetle-headed."

Knowing that her brother was witnessing her embarrassment only made her blush deeper and she turned her face away. Soft blonde curls tickled her cheeks, falling gently down her neck and along the threads of her shawl.

"I am well. It is quite hot in here, is it not?" she replied, looking about for a fan. Of course, it was December and there was no need for such an instrument.

"Perhaps you are merely excited," Xavier teased, peering down at her with intelligent green eyes.

"Excited?" she repeated. "About what?"

Xavier leered and laughed again, shaking his own blonde mane with glee.

"You need not be coy with me, Emmy. I am your only brother. I know what happens in this hotel as well as you do."

Emmeline stared at him blankly, trying to reconcile what he could possibly mean.

"For the gala tomorrow?" she offered although she could not fathom why Xavier would consider that an exciting prospect. Parties were hardly affairs to be celebrated as a Balfour. She would spend her evening dancing with her father's associates and having trite conversations with women who cared more about the latest fashions than they did their own offspring.

Xavier's smile faded slightly and he cocked his head to the side.

"You truly do not know?" he asked and the manner in which he posed the question caused shivers of concern through Emmeline's delicate form.

"Xavy, please, do not keep me in suspense," she murmured. "What is it?"

She hoped it was not something for which she would be required to prepare a great deal.

I do loathe surprises. What has Father done now?

Xavier sighed and chuckled.

"You need not be so worried, my dear. It is good news indeed."

She waited as he grinned broadly and reached for her gloved hand, leaning in closely to whisper loudly.

"Tomorrow night, at the ball, Walter will ask for your hand in marriage before all of Luton."

Emmeline reeled back in shock, her fingers slipping out of her brother's grasp.

"What?" she choked. "Whatever do you mean?"

It was Xavier's turn to appear confused and his beaming grin disappeared.

"You do not seem happy," he commented. "I thought you would be more joyful about the news."

"Joyful?" she repeated. "How can I be joyful when I do not even know the man I am to marry except that he is…"

She trailed off and looked about, lest someone overhear her disparaging remarks about Walter Greene.

"He and Father have discussed it several times over the past months," Xavier explained, his eyes darkening. "I assumed Mr. Greene had spoken to you also."

Emmeline's mouth gaped open but nary a noise emitted.

"Emmy? Do say something."

But what was there to say? She had always known that one day, she would be betrothed to a man whom met her father's approval, but Walter Greene? The idea caused her to shudder.

"I-I must speak to Father," she whispered, turning blindly toward the lobby.

"Do not tell him I told you!" Xavier yelled out after her, causing the guests to scowl at his rudeness but Emmeline was far too distracted to apologize for her boisterous brother.

I do not wish to marry Mr. Greene or anyone else for that matter, she thought desperately, making her way toward her father's office next to the concierge desk. *But most certainly not Mr. Greene. How can Father do this to me?*

There was only one way to know and that was to confront Charlton Balfour before the engagement occurred.

"Miss Balfour, he is not to be disturbed," Matthew informed her from the counter as she swept through toward his office. "However, your mother is in her quarters."

Emmeline paused and looked to the boy at the desk, her mind whirling as she considered ignoring him and bursting through to confront her father about the arrangement he had made.

Of course Mother is in her quarters. She is always in her quarters.

"Thank you, Matthew," she muttered, turning away from the office to take the center stairs up to her mother's chambers.

If I cannot see Father, perhaps I can plead with Mother, if only to gain myself time in the matter.

It was a ridiculous idea, but given her state of mind, Emmeline could think of nothing else to do but sit by and be idle, something which she did not handle well.

I must do something. Hopefully Mother is coherent enough to help me through this.

As Matthew had dictated, Anne Balfour sat at her vanity, brushing her blonde tresses. It was not difficult to see where her children had inherited their comely appearance. Even at five and forty, Anne was a lovely woman, not a strand of white amongst her golden crown. Small wrinkles had begun to show themselves at the corners of her luminous green eyes, but Anne was still very much the beauty she had always been.

"Your mother was the comeliest lass in all of Luton," Charlton often told the children when they were young. "I was the only one who could afford her dowry."

How long has it been since he has spun that yarn to us? Emmeline thought wistfully. It had been a long while since Charlton had spoken well of his wife at all, to Emmeline's recollection.

It has been a long while for many things in this household, Emmeline thought with some bitterness.

"Mother, may I enter?" she asked quietly from the salon. Anne waved a heavily ringed hand without speaking and Emmeline stepped in to join her in the bedchamber, sliding the doors between the sitting room closed for privacy.

"Before you speak a word, Emmeline, I am in no mood for theatrics today, am I clear?"

Emmeline supressed a sharp retort, knowing that it would not benefit her to protest.

When is she ever in the mood for theatrics? If Mother had her way, she would never leave her quarters. We barely see her as it is.

Once, Anne had graced the halls with her luxurious gowns and charming smiles, wooing the guests with her easy disposition and witty banter. Gradually, however, she had let the hotel slip away as she turned to seek solace for whatever was plaguing her soul in the bottom of a sherry decanter.

If Emmeline were to consider when things had gone awry with her mother, she could never quite find the precise moment in time. It seemed that one day she was a vibrant, sparkling woman, and the next an inconsolable drunk.

Charlton had barely seemed to notice, simply replacing his wife with Emmeline for the purposes of acting as hostess of the hotel. Emmeline had been young enough not to realize she had taken her mother's place, not until it was too late and she was the new face of the Balfour Hotel. Sometimes, Emmeline wondered if her mother resented her and if her animus was the cause of Anne's misery.

"Mother, I must speak to you about my engagement," Emmeline told her breathlessly, sliding down to crouch at Anne's side. "I knew nothing of it!"

"Your engagement?" Anne asked nonchalantly, dropping the silver-handled brush against the toilet. She did not meet her daughter's eyes and Emmeline was filled with a new sense of foreboding. The smell of alcohol wafted toward Emmeline and she sank back onto her haunches before trying again to reason with her mother.

"Mother, I understand I must be married, but to Walter Greene?" she insisted. "Surely there are better matches?"

"I do not interject myself in business matters, Emmeline," Anne told her, still averting her eyes as she dusted her face with powder. "You must learn to do the same, particularly if you wish for the guests to like you. Smile and accept."

As if to accentuate her point, Anne beamed at herself eerily in the mirror as though she was greeting guests.

"I...Mother, this is not a business matter," Emmeline cried, frustration mounting inside her. "This is my marriage."

Finally, Anne pivoted her head and peered at her. The older woman's mouth became a fine line of disapproval.

"Is there a difference?" Her mother asked dully. Emmeline scoffed indignantly.

THE HEIRESS'S SECRET LOVE

"Sincerely, Mother? Of course there is!"

"Emmeline, be sensible for once in your life. You are a woman now and you must act accordingly." Anne all but threw her hands up in exasperation.

"Mother, you are not speaking sense. I am discussing my engagement and you are talking about the hotel."

Anne snorted unbecomingly and shook her head in disgust.

"I blame your father," she muttered. "He spoiled you. You and Xavier. Indulged your every whim and now look at you!"

It was not yet nine o'clock in the morning and Emmeline knew her mother was ape-drunk already.

Ballocks, she thought, although she did not dare speak such vile cant aloud. *She will be useless to help my cause.*

"You should rest, Mother," Emmeline sighed, rising to her feet. "I will speak with Father."

"You bloody fool!" Anne howled. "Have you not heard a word I just spoke?"

Emmeline stared at her mother with pity. She knew she should have never bothered Anne with such matters. Anne did not know one day from the next. It was foolish of Emmeline to have come.

"Of course I heard you, Mother. You rest," she murmured, turning away. Abruptly, Anne began to laugh.

"You may speak to your father, Emmeline but his answer will be the same as the one I just gave you. Your marriage is business, girl. They are one in the same. He is marrying you to Walter Greene because it is what is best for the hotel."

Emmeline blinked several times, the truth of Anne's words stinging her like a dagger penetrating her heart.

She is not confused. I am.

"You are nothing more than a commodity for the hotel, Emmeline, a notation on the accompts. You will marry whomever your father deems fit."

The words sickened Emmeline, not because they were laced with the bitter venom of an unstable woman, but because she knew them to be a fact.

It was the only reason that her father would have kept the betrothal from her.

He does not care about my opinion on the matter, nor my happiness. It is irrelevant. I am irrelevant.

CHAPTER TWO

Elias wiped away the sweat forming on his brow and kept his eyes trained on Honor Wesley as he knew the maître d' watched him with as much intensity.

You very nearly ruined it, he chided himself for the umpteenth time since arriving at the hotel. Again, he was forced to remember that he was still there, on the property.

"Elias," Honor barked. "What do you do in this situation?"

Elias shifted his eyes toward the table and looked about for anything that appeared to be amiss.

"I would fetch another fork and ensure the guest is comfortable," Elias replied quickly.

"You do not speak to the guest unless he speaks to you first," Honor told the new waiters, neither commending nor disapproving of Elias' suggestion. "You are to be seen and not heard."

Through the corner of his eye, he noted that the other waiters hung off Honor's words but Elias was less concerned with learning restaurant etiquette than he was about knowing the employees.

The chambermaids had disappeared with Antoinette leaving the men inside the now-vacant dining room to train for lunch and dinner services. Elias was eager to move freely throughout the building, but he knew he had already called far too much attention to himself by arriving late.

"Elias, you will tend to the room bells with Joshua." Honor's voice brought him back again and Elias nodded instinctively.

"As you wish, Mr. Wesley."

"Come along," a sandy haired boy whispered, nudging his arm. "You are fortunate getting such service on your first day."

"Am I?" Elias asked pleasantly, following Joshua toward the kitchen, he noticed everything around them as they walked, his mind processing the surroundings as though he might find a clue to what he was seeking among the artfully decorated dining room.

"I am Joshua Milner. I was born here at The Balfour," the blonde boy explained, his voice light and happy. "My mother and father worked here until they passed and my grandfather too."

Elias looked at the boy, gauging his age to be no more than nineteen.

"You seem pleased about that," Elias commented. Joshua paused and stared at him with wide eyes.

"You must know this is the best hotel in which to work. You said yourself that you traveled from Peterborough to be here."

"You heard that?" Elias asked, slightly uncomfortable.

"Everyone heard that," Joshua laughed. "I daresay that Miss Balfour had tears in her eyes."

"Miss Balfour? The owner's daughter?" Elias asked as they continued into the kitchen.

"Yes. She was there for your impassioned speech also."

Elias was instantly reminded of the finely dressed woman who had stood in the shadows and his heart leaped unexpectedly.

"Yes," he murmured. "I saw her there."

"She is very kind," Joshua told him confidentially, lowering his voice. "She treats us as though we are more than just servants."

Elias stopped at a long rectangular table and Joshua nodded to him to sit, pointing up at the wall. A series of bells hung, forty in total, each connected to a number.

"When a bell tolls, we must run to the respective room to attend to the guest. Never can this table be left unoccupied. God forbid the

Duke of Workenshire be without his cigarettes for more than a moment."

"What if there are multiple bells tolling at once?" Elias wished to know and Joshua grinned disarmingly.

"You will quickly learn who is the most important. The fifth floor is for the Balfours and their ilk. You will always tend to them first. The second floor houses the poorer of the rich who come. The third and fourth floors will invariably house the peers and wealthy merchants from abroad."

"I assume that means I should always ignore the second floor until the others are cared for."

Joshua's face brightened more, if that were possible, and he nodded eagerly.

"You are a quick study!" he cried, clapping Elias on the back heartily and the older man realized that he liked Joshua immediately.

It will be important to make friends like him, he thought. *He has extensive knowledge of this hotel and he is amiable enough.*

"Tell me, Joshua—"

"You may call me Josh. All my friends do," the boy interjected and Elias offered him a genuine smile.

"Josh. Are you well acquainted with the staff, then?"

He shrugged and flopped unceremoniously into a chair at Elias' side.

"We live in close quarters," Joshua explained. "Many of us are the children of previous staff."

"Do you know—" Elias did not have an opportunity to finish his question as a bell began to chime above their heads.

"Oh! That is the master suite—Mrs. Balfour. I will go." Joshua rose but Elias stopped him.

"Allow me," he insisted to Joshua's surprise. "I will never learn if I do not try."

Joshua looked to him warily.

"I agree," he muttered. "But I should forewarn you—Mrs. Balfour does enjoy her cups. She can be rather...unpredictable at times."

"I appreciate your candor," Elias told him, hurrying as the chime of the bell grew more insistent. "I will exercise caution."

Before Joshua could say another word, Elias hurried toward the servant's stairs and made his way to the fifth floor in a shockingly short time.

If you are to run these stairs multiple times a day, you will need to conserve your stamina, Elias told himself, but his eagerness to explore the hotel was motivating him to move at a greater speed than he typically would have.

How inane a thought. You would not be here under typical circumstances.

The application he had submitted to serve at the Balfour Hotel had been that of sheer fiction, fabrications he had created in bits and pieces from others' lives whom he had met along the way. In fact, Elias Compton had never waited on any guest at any hotel in his eight and twenty years of life.

Yet, as Joshua says, I am a quick study.

Elias knew he had little choice in the matter. He could not foil his plan, not when he was so close to finding the answers he sought.

He rounded the corner from the stairs and collided with a body as he did, the two falling apart in a gasp of shock.

"Pardon me!" Elias cried, righting himself immediately. His face paled when he saw who it was he had bumped.

"Forgive me," Miss Balfour muttered, smoothing the skirt of her dress. "I was paying no mind to where I was walking."

Elias stared at her, noting the unusually pasty palor of her skin. She certainly had not seemed so wan when he had seen her earlier that morning.

"Are you well, Miss Balfour? Is there something I could fetch for you?" he asked with concern. She appeared to be breathing shortly and, as he looked to her hands, it was clear they were trembling.

"No, no," she muttered, turning her head away. "I am..."

Abruptly, her eyes shifted back toward him and their gazes caught and locked just as they had earlier in the kitchen.

"Oh!" she breathed. "You are here."

A pink tinge touched her cheeks as she spoke and Elias watched as she shifted her eyes away.

"I mean to say that you have been hired."

"Yes, Miss. Elias Compton, at your service."

"Emmeline Balfour."

To his shock, she extended her hand and he stared at it, unsure if he was being taunted by the white glove. Joshua's words rang through his ears.

"She is very kind. She treats us as though we are more than just servants."

He accepted her palm quickly and bowed his head, knowing that if he was caught, regardless of her introduction, he would be terminated without question.

"Welcome to the Balfour Hotel. I hope you will be very happy here."

"Thank you, Miss Balfour."

"Emmeline," she murmured and his eyes widened again.

"Pardon, Miss?"

"Never mind," she sighed, gathering her skirts. "Forgive me, Mr. Compton. I have matters to attend to at the moment but I do hope we will have an opportunity to speak again. I would like very much to know about your life in Peterborough."

Elias was inexplicably pleased that she had remembered from where he hailed but he warned himself not to think too deeply about her words.

It is her business to involve herself in the comings and goings of the staff, he reasoned even though he was not certain that was so. There was a gleam in her eye, one that radiated more interest than that of an employer to an employee.

You have no business with the likes of Emmeline Balfour, he growled to himself even as he answered, "I would enjoy that also, Miss Balfour."

She did not move, her amber-green eyes narrowing slightly as though she was attempting to recall something quite on the edge of her thoughts but she shook her head to shake it away.

"Until then," she said, her voice like warm honey.

Can any woman be so lovely and so kind?

"Good day."

He watched as she shuffled past him, using the servant's stairs and again surprising Elias with her humility.

She certainly does not act as though she is the daughter of the owner of the Balfour. I wonder why she has not yet married.

He forced his feet to move toward Anne Balfour's chambers. Even as he knocked on the door and tried to refocus his thoughts on the job before him, he could not get the image of Emmeline Balfour from his mind.

————

Joshua chuckled when Elias returned to the kitchen.

"I see she did not go easily upon you," Joshua jeered and Elias managed a wry smile.

"You did not fib. She is quite..." Elias did not wish to finish his thought aloud but Joshua spared him the word.

"Saucy, I do believe is what you are pining to say," Joshua snickered. "I have yet to see that woman without a cup pressed to her mouth. What does she require? Is her decanter empty already? It is not even ten o'clock!"

"She is hungry," Elias sighed, nodding toward one of the cooks with his order for the lady of the hotel. He turned back to Joshua who had reclaimed his seat against the massive table used to feed the staff.

"Joshua, I have a question to ask of you," Elias told him and the boy looked to him eagerly.

"You may ask me anything. I know this hotel better than even the Balfours," he boasted and Elias believed him. He was, in fact, depending upon that.

"Do you know of a chambermaid named Christiana?" Elias asked, lowering his voice lest the other staff overhear him. Joshua's eyebrows rose in surprise.

"She was fired for stealing not three months past," Joshua replied. "Pity that. I rather liked her. Compared to some of the other abigails in this monstrosity, I daresay she was quite pleasant. But, the pay is not so good."

"Stealing?" Elias choked. "Christiana?"

"It happens a fair bit. You should not be so shocked."

Suddenly, Joshua stared at him, his face paling.

"You share the same surname," Joshua muttered. "Are you related to her?"

Elias pressed his index finger to his mouth and looked about furtively.

"You mustn't tell anyone," Elias hissed quietly.

"W-why are you here?" Joshua asked nervously. "If Mr. Wesley learns that you are related to a thief…"

"I find it impossible to believe Christiana would steal a scrap of discarded food," Elias growled. "Something else has happened to her."

"How can you be certain?" Joshua insisted.

"If she was fired, she would have written or returned home but I have not heard a word from her in three months."

"Perhaps she was embarrassed and wanted to spare your family the shame."

A mirthless smile touched Elias' mouth.

"I assure you, Christiana would not have done that."

"This may be difficult to accept, Elias but siblings are not always how we recall them in their youth. Perhaps this time apart has brought forth the devil in her—"

"She is not my sister," Elias sighed, sitting back and shaking his head.

"Oh…your cousin then?"

"No," Elias grunted. "She is my wife."

CHAPTER THREE

"He is still occupied, Miss Balfour," Matthew explained. "Shall I have him send for you when he is done?"

"With whom is he in conference?" Emmeline asked, trying to peer through the glass but the curtains were drawn.

"Mr. Greene, Miss Balfour."

The mere sound of his name made her blood run cold. She stepped away from the concierge desk.

"I will return. Do not tell my father I was seeking him," she told Matthew, spinning toward the kitchen. She wished the day had not taken on such a bitterness. She longed to go for a walk and clear her mind.

I am not thinking rationally, she thought, sauntering aimlessly through the busy galley.

The clanging of pots and pans was often cathartic to Emmeline's ears, a soothing chaos somehow. It reminded her of childhood, the same scents tantalizing her nostrils as she moved through the steaming kitchen to stand off in the shadows alone.

"You look as though you are thoroughly enjoying that spot."

She glanced over her shoulder and laughed nervously as she realized that Elias Compton stood at her back.

"I did not see you there, Mr. Compton."

"You may call me Elias, Miss Balfour. It is your right."

She nodded.

"All right, Elias," she agreed, facing him fully. "Has Honor demoted you to the kitchen now?"

He chuckled at her jest.

"Not yet, Miss but there is time. I fear he has been watching me quite closely since I arrived."

"You must not take it personally, Elias. This hotel is the most prestigious in these parts and Honor does take his duties quite seriously. I daresay, if he did not like you, he would not have hired you at all."

"I will take your advisement on the matter, Miss Balfour."

He moved past her.

"I should get back to work before he realizes I have snuck away."

"Why have you snuck away?" she called after him. "Is the work too much?"

"No, Miss," he replied quickly. "I was merely warming myself by the hearth."

He vanished into the crowd of servants and Emmeline found herself watching after him. It was not until she heard a slight grunt at her side that she turned her head to peer at another waiter.

"Good morrow, Josh. Are you well?" she asked sweetly.

"Yes, Miss Balfour," he muttered but Emmeline could see that something troubled him.

"Is there a matter?"

He swallowed visibly and shook his head. Emmeline did not believe him.

"Joshua, we used to run amok together," she reminded him gently. "I daresay you have even pulled my hair. There is nothing you cannot tell me."

He looked at her uncertainly and again moved his eyes away.

"I-it is not my place, Miss Balfour," he mumbled, his eyes trained on the ground. "But as you say, we have a long history."

"Then do speak freely. I can assure you of my confidences."

He inhaled and looked over his shoulder, in the direction where Elias had gone.

"It is the new waiter, Miss Balfour. I fear that he has come here with bad intentions."

Defensiveness fused through Emmeline, though she could not say why. She had no reason to doubt Joshua. On the contrary, in fact. She regarded him as almost kin and yet his words bothered her greatly.

She held in her thoughts and peered at him speculatively.

"What basis have you for such a claim?"

He fiddled nervously with his fingers and smoothed back his hair quickly, all while keeping his eyes averted.

"Miss Balfour, he confessed to me that he is here in search of Christiana Compton."

Of course! Compton. I knew I recalled the name!

"She is no longer employed here, am I correct?" Emmeline replied, trying to recall the last time she had seen the dark-haired woman about the hotel. "It has been a few months, has it not?"

"Yes, Miss Balfour..."

Emmeline waited expectantly.

"What is it?"

"She was fired for stealing, Miss."

Emmeline suddenly understood Joshua's conflict.

"I see," she murmured. "And now her kin has come to work here. Has he explained why?"

"I feel rather disloyal speaking like this," Joshua breathed as though he only then realized that he would be unable to retract his words. "Forgive me, Miss Balfour for he seems like a decent enough chap."

"But you question his presence. I do not think you an unreasonable sort. Why has he come?"

"He claims he has not heard from Christiana in months and has come to locate her."

"Perhaps she does not wish to be found."

"I had suggested the same, Miss but he was adamant that it was not natural for her to go without word."

"I fear we do not know our family as well as we sometimes hope," Emmeline sighed.

"I also said as much," Joshua replied, sounding relieved that he had absolution in the matter. "I feel foolish for bringing this to you, Miss Balfour, but I did see him speaking with you and I felt you should know that his heart is not in the hotel or the guests."

Emmeline's lips pressed firmly together as she considered what to do next. She remembered how desperate Elias had sounded to be given a chance at the job, despite his late arrival.

Whatever his reasons, he genuinely wishes to be here. Should I end this charade or simply permit it to work itself out?

"I have given you another burden to manage," Joshua sighed. "Forgive me, Miss."

"This is not a burden and you need not apologize. What good am I if not to resolve issues pertaining to the hotel?"

"I cannot say this is an issue," Joshua said, worry clouding his features, but Emmeline smiled at him reassuringly.

"You need not worry, Josh. I will handle the matter delicately and with discretion. Your name need not come into the matter at all."

"Thank you, Miss Balfour. You are too kind."

He bowed and moved away as Emmeline pondered what she had been told.

What had come of Christiana Compton?

If anyone would know, it would be Antoinette.

————

Emmeline found the housekeeper on the third floor, overseeing her chambermaids wearing her usual pinched expression.

"There, Cora. You are missing the corners as always."

"Yes, Mrs. Baxter."

"Antoinette, may I have a word with you?" Emmeline asked.

"Certainly, Miss Balfour. Is everything well?"

"I have a question for you about a maid who worked here not three months past."

"I fear we have had a rather high turnaround in the past months, Miss Balfour. You must be more specific."

"Christiana Compton. Do you recall her? She was Mrs. Balfour's abigail for a time, was she not?"

A darkness fell over Antoinette's expressions and her mouth thinned into a tight line.

"Yes."

Emmeline stared at her expectantly.

"What became of her?"

"She was terminated."

"For what cause?"

"Stealing, if I recall. Should you wish to know more, you must speak with your father about the matter, Miss Balfour. He was directly responsible for ending her employment. Is there another matter?"

Emmeline blinked at the abrupt dismissal, a peculiar niggling arising from her gut.

"Is that commonplace?" Emmeline asked, refusing to let the matter go, despite Antoinette's reluctance to continue to discuss it.

"Pardon?"

"My father does not often get involved in the affairs of the maids. Why was he the one to relieve her of her duties?"

Antoinette turned her head, pretending to examine the servants' work but Emmeline knew the woman well enough to know she was avoiding the question.

"I could not say, Miss Balfour but in this instance, he did."

Rudely, Antoinette walked away and Emmeline gaped after her.

Is she lying to me or hiding something?

"My word, you are impossible to find some days," Xavier grumbled, appearing at the end of the hall. "Father is looking for you."

"Is he? How interesting. I was seeking him too."

She followed her brother along the halls and he cast her a nervous look.

"You spoke with Mother about the betrothal," he sighed and Emmeline stopped walking.

"I did."

"I wish you had not."

Anger flashed through her.

"What would you have me do?"

Xavier exhaled heavily and faced his sister.

"This is not the place to discuss this, Emmy but I do know you are overwhelmed. When you speak with Father, do try to keep your wits about you. Dissolving into a fit of histrionics will solve nothing."

"According to Mother, there is nothing to be solved. The matter is done."

"That may well be, Emmy but why do you protest? Surely you knew you were to be wed one day."

"One day, yes and I had hoped to a man who had made some effort to court me. Instead, I have been, what, bid off like a prized pig at auction?"

"Emmy, keep your tone down."

Instantly, she did as she was told, knowing that was precisely the behavior her brother was warning her against.

"I realize it is not ideal for you," he told her again. "If it were up to me, I would see you married to a duke but Father seems to think that Walter Greene has attributes that some others do not."

"I am not disputing that this marriage will be what is proper for the hotel. I am disputing that it will be proper for me!"

"Emmy..."

"I know, Xavier. You need not placate me. I know my duties and I will fulfill them by marrying that rogue if need be."

She spun toward the stairs and jumped as she again came face-to-face with Elias Compton.

How much did he hear?

"Pardon me," she muttered, brushing by him.

"Miss Balfour. Mr. Xavier," Elias mumbled, lowering his head but as she moved, Emmeline did manage to catch his eye one final time. Was it her imagination or was there really an unmistakable disappointment in the depths of their glowing aquamarine.

Is he upset that I am to be married? She wondered as she made her way down the stairs. The idea was ludicrous and yet it oddly filled Emmeline with the tiniest bit of hope—the most she had felt all day.

And what of it? What if Elias Compton is devastated that I am to wed Walter Greene? It is not as though he would ever be in the position to court me.

A newly familiar blush stained her cheeks as she glided into the lobby and stood before her father's office.

Can you imagine the scandal? A waiter pursuing an heiress. The gossips would never cease!

The more she considered it, the more it tickled her and suddenly, Emmeline's mind was back on the third floor with Elias, staring once more into his intense eyes.

She heard Xavier descend behind her and she quickly regained her composure.

"Shall we?" her brother asked. She looked to him as he extended his arm for her to take but suddenly, Emmeline had no desire to see her father at all.

"No," she replied, turning away before Charlton could see her. "Tell Father you could not find me."

"Emmy!"

"I will seek him out later," she promised, rushing toward the staircase, almost falling over the hem of her skirts, but before she could vanish onto the second floor, Charlton Balfour's voice rang out.

"No," he boomed. "You will see me now."

Begrudgingly, Emmeline turned back, grinding her teeth together.

"You cannot disrupt this hotel at your convenience, Emmeline," Charlton told her in a low tone. "Enter at once."

For a brief, defiant moment, she considered fleeing, but to what end? Eventually, she would have to face her father and deal with the facts of her engagement.

You are using Elias Compton as a distraction, she told herself, shuffling back down the stairs to meet her family. *Put him out of your mind before you do something foolish.*

CHAPTER FOUR

She is to be engaged.

The information left Elias stunned well after Emmeline had disappeared with her brother to the lower levels of the hotel. He knew he should not care, that the proprietor's daughter had no bearing on his life. Or so he would continue to tell himself.

Your business here is to find your own wife, he reminded himself. *You need not concern yourself with the affairs of another's betrothal.*

Elias wondered then, why he could not shake the growing jealousy inside him.

"Have you not matters to attend to, Elias?"

Antoinette's sharp tone brought him back to the present and he lowered his eyes shamefully.

"Yes, madam," he replied, pushing the tea cart forward. "I merely had something in my eye."

"If your disposition is so weak that you cannot forge through a simple dust mote, you may have to rethink your employment here," the head housekeeper snapped. "Do not let me catch you being idle again."

"Yes, Mrs. Baxter."

He hurried past her, carefully avoiding her withering stare as he did.

You have caused too much of a stir on your first day. You must do better, be stealthier.

Elias considered what he had told Joshua earlier about his true reasons for being at the hotel and he wondered if he had made a mistake. It was too late for regret, but Elias was aware of his blunder.

I do hope that Joshua can be trusted.

He paused to knock at the door of room 303.

"Who is there?" a gruff voice called out and Elias cleared his throat.

"Lunch, Mr. Greene, as per your request."

Abruptly, the door flew inward and Elias was faced with a remarkably gruff-looking man, thick in stature with a pock-marked face.

"How long does it take one to fetch a stew?" he snarled, spinning away from the door to saunter inside, his stout legs thumping across the floor toward the sitting room.

"Forgive the delay, Mr. Greene," Elias replied, examining the man through his peripheral vision. He was not what Elias had expected.

Could this be the same Mr. Greene who is to marry Emmeline? If so, I can certainly understand her reluctance. The man is sour-faced and beau-nasty in appearance. Even with his fine clothing, he is unkempt.

"Will you take all day?" Mr. Greene demanded. "I would like to eat before I perish of hunger."

Elias could see there was little fear of any such occurrence, what with Mr. Greene's portly belly nearly bursting from his black waistcoat.

"Yes, sir."

Elias set the tray evenly in the middle of the heavy carpeted room and removed the silver lids from the plates before moving aside to wait for the older man's approval.

"That will do," Walter Greene barked. "Off with you now."

Elias bowed his head and backed out of the room without another word but not without casting the man another covert look.

The idea that the dainty and delicate Emmeline Balfour could wed such a brute was inconceivable. Despite Walter Greene's expensive dress, there was an edge of cant in his speech as though he had not been reared in wealth.

Who is this man and why would Charlton Balfour accept him as family when his daughter could easily be wed to royalty with her standing and grace?

He made his way back down through the hotel to return to his post before the bells.

Joshua was no longer there but he did encounter Honor Wesley.

"Have you found your way?" the maître d' asked.

"I have, Mr. Wesley, thank you."

"Tell me, Elias, are you related to Christiana Compton?"

His face paled at the question and he gaped at his superior, uncertain if he should lie.

"Did Joshua speak with you?" Elias asked, realizing that was what must have transpired. To his chagrin, Honor's eyes darkened.

"Joshua knows of this?" he demanded and Elias stifled a wince of regret.

"You must not fault him, Mr. Wesley. I have not come here with mal intent," Elias told him quietly, his teal eyes darting about nervously. "I only wish to know what happened to my wife."

"Your wife?" Honor echoed, his eyes growing wide with alarm. "She was married?"

A prickle of apprehension slid through Elias.

"She *is* wed to me, yes," he replied slowly. "Has she not mentioned it?"

"I do not associate with the chambermaids, Elias. All I know for certain is that she is no longer here. If your only reason for coming is to find your wife, I suggest you pack your belongings and leave at once."

"I will not leave until I know what became of Christiana," Elias told him firmly. "I will do my job but I cannot simply go without answers, Mr. Wesley."

Honor's eyes narrowed.

"And what do you suppose Mr. Balfour will say when he discovers that there is a spy on staff?"

"A spy?" Elias repeated. "What bearing does my presence have on such an important man?"

"You cannot stay," Honor told him flatly. "I will not have you disrupt the hotel with your theories."

Confusion swept through Elias.

"What theories?" he demanded. "All I know is that I have not heard from Christiana in months and she would not simply disappear."

"Perhaps you do not know her as well as you think."

Elias was growing weary at being told the same thing but he held the protest on his tongue.

"Mr. Wesley, please. Do give me a week to learn where she might have gone and I assure you, I will cause no disruption to the hotel. You cannot afford to lose a waiter so close to the yule season and it will take you as long to find a replacement for me. Please."

"No."

The flatness in his tone was unnerving.

"Do not make me escort you from the property, Mr. Compton. Gather you belongings and leave at once."

Honor did not grant him the opportunity to respond as he spun away, but Elias did not move from his place.

There was nothing he could do but leave as instructed and he was no closer to solving the mystery of his missing wife than he had been upon his arrival.

Oh Christiana, what have you done now? He thought mournfully. *Why must I spend my life protecting you?*

It was not the first time he had been enacted to care for his wife and Elias had long since accepted that it was the life to which he had committed but it did not grow any less tiresome with the years.

He had been vehemently opposed to Christiana leaving Peterborough to work at the Balfour Hotel, but like all else in her life, she did whatever she pleased, packing her belongings in the night and leaving when Elias had been asleep.

Of course she had written him to let her husband know she was safe and employed. It was not as though Elias wanted nor needed a single pence from her, but he did long for Christiana to return home where he could watch her, lest she find herself in peril—once more.

It was inevitable that he was forced to come look for her. In his heart, Elias knew that she would invariably find some way to endanger herself and there he was, chasing ghosts.

Sighing, Elias knew he had no choice but to leave the hotel.

Unless I find somewhere to hide…

He loathed that it had come to this, that his existence had been centered around the frivolous whims of Christiana, but Elias also realized that until he saw her with his own eyes, he could not simply return to Peterborough.

"Elias, the bell to the office has been tolling for almost a minute," Joshua grunted. "What in God's name are you doing?"

He moved his eyes toward the younger man and frowned.

"I have been relieved of my position," he informed Joshua. "I fear you will need to tend to whatever it is Mr. Balfour requires."

"Relieved?" Joshua echoed, his complexion waning. "By Miss Balfour?"

"Why would Miss Balfour…oh…" Disappointment filled Elias and he nodded slowly. "You told her who I was."

"Forgive me, Elias! My loyalty has always been to this hotel and the Balfours. You seem to be a decent fellow but if something were to happen—"

Elias held up his hand and shook his head.

"You need not explain," he told the boy. "I should not have put you in such a position. I am the only one to blame, thinking my ploy could succeed. I am merely at my wit's end, Josh."

Joshua made a commiserating noise and looked nervously toward the bell which continued to chime.

"When must you leave?" he asked.

"Immediately. Do not allow me to keep you. You need not be terminated also," Elias urged him. "Thank you for being kind to me."

Elias turned away but Joshua called out to him.

"Wait!"

"What is it?"

"You may stay in my chambers until my shift is done. I will help you find Christiana."

Elias' jaw slackened slightly and he began to shake his head.

"I cannot ask that of you, Josh. You are already conflicted about this."

"I made a mistake revealing your secret to Miss Balfour. I can see that you are a good man, merely looking for your wife."

Oh...did he tell Emmeline Balfour that I was married?

The notion caused the bile to rise in the back of his throat, even if it was the truth.

You have truly made a mess of your affairs when you agreed to this life with Christiana.

"I have put you in a terrible circumstance, choosing between a stranger and your home," Elias told him. "If you are caught—"

"I will not be," Joshua assured him quickly. "I have my own quarters and I know the schedule of the staff well. Wait there for me and we will discuss this more later. But please, go now before we are both discovered. I will not be of any use to you if I, too, am thrown out of the hotel."

Joshua smiled disarmingly to take the seriousness from his words and scampered toward the office.

He is truly your only ally here and I do not believe he meant any harm by telling Miss Balfour your affairs.

Elias hurried toward the staff quarters, keeping his head low as he moved.

I wonder why Miss Balfour did not speak to me about my presence, he thought but he remembered the conversation he had overheard between her and her brother.

It was clear to see that Emmeline had more pressing matters on her mind and rightfully so.

Will she truly marry that beast of a man, Walter Greene?

Elias prayed to God that the answer was no, even though he fully knew he had no future of his own with the beautiful blonde heiress.

That does not mean that she does not deserve happiness, Elias told himself firmly. He wondered if there was a way he could ensure that Emmeline received it.

CHAPTER FIVE

"Where is the blasted waiter?" Xavier mumbled, pacing about the office. Emmeline wished he would sit. His moving about only fueled her apprehension beneath her father's scathing stare.

"Sit down, Xavier," Charlton snapped. "Your scotch will keep."

Reluctantly, Xavier joined his father and sister at the desk and sank into the seat but not before ringing the service bell one last time.

"The staff in this hotel is growing lazy," Xavier grumbled and Emmeline could not help but wonder if one of the new waiters was coming.

Perhaps Elias Compton.

Shamed that she was thinking about the handsome serving boy when her future hung in the balance, Emmeline dropped her head.

"What cause did you have for upsetting your mother this morning, Emmy?" Charlton demanded. "If you have a matter, you know better than to alarm your mother."

"You were otherwise engaged," Emmeline replied evenly. "I did come to you first."

"Then you wait until I will see you. What did you hope to accomplish by complaining to your mother about your betrothal?"

"What betrothal?" Emmeline barked back. "I knew nothing of this!

Forgive my shock to learn I would be blindsided at the ball tomorrow but how would you expect me to react, Father?"

"With the decorum of a Balfour as your breeding dictates!" Charlton snarled back. "Certainly not by upsetting your mother in her fragile condition."

Emmeline chewed on her tongue to keep from asking when being a drunk was considered fragility.

"What is the issue, daughter? I have promised you to a man of good standing, one who will provide for you and this hotel as I see fit."

"Walter Greene, Father? The man is hardly..."

Charlton's eyes narrowed.

"Hardly what, Emmeline? He has been beneficial in ways that I do not need explain to you. You will do as you are told and I will not hear another word on the matter."

Emmeline tried to hold the anger from her face, but she knew it shone through with clarity.

Mother was right after all.

"I suppose the matter is settled then," she replied stiffly, rising from her chair. "I imagine you have work to attend to."

There was a gentle knock at the door and Joshua appeared.

"You rang, sir?"

"I rang, Josh but I believe our interview has concluded," Xavier said quickly as Emmeline glided out of the office, blinking the indignation from her eyes.

Walter Greene. He may be wealthy but his reputation as a rogue and a scoundrel precedes him. I know nothing of the man on a personal level but the idea of marrying such a hideous, amoral man...

She shuddered but before she made her way to the stairwell, Joshua reached her side.

"Miss Balfour," he murmured. "May I speak with you privately?"

Emmeline stifled a sigh and peered at him. She was in no mood to speak to anyone, but the pleading in his face made her pause.

"Of course," she agreed, forcing a smile. "What is it?"

He nodded toward the corner of the lobby and they moved into a discrete area.

"Elias Compton has been let go of his position," Joshua told her quietly. "Did you order this?"

Shame flooded his face and he looked away as if the words said aloud humiliated him.

"Of course," he rushed on. "It is within your right and I dare not question your authority."

Emmeline felt a pang of surprise.

"Certainly not!" she replied. "I had nothing to do with his termination. Where is he now?"

"He has been ordered from the hotel," Joshua explained and a panic flooded her.

"By whom? Why?" she cried. The idea that she might not see him again troubled her a great deal more than she could comprehend.

I do not know him and yet...

"I...Miss, I asked him to wait in my chambers until we could speak privately. I only wished to ensure that you did not have him expelled from the hotel on my account."

"Your chambers?" she repeated. "I will speak to him myself. Now."

She gathered her skirts to turn and retreat, but spun back around, pausing as she stared at her father's office.

Father fired Christiana Compton. I will speak to him first.

"Please, Miss Balfour," Joshua called out in a loud whisper. "I know I have broken the rules but he seems genuinely concerned for his wife's welfare."

A wave of solid ice fell over Emmeline and she pivoted to look into Joshua's face.

"His *wife*?" she echoed. "Christiana is his wife?"

A perplexed look crossed over Joshua's face and he nodded slowly.

"Did I not mention that previously?"

"You did not."

"Oh...well, yes...does that much matter?"

Emmeline regained her composure and shook her regal head quickly.

"Of course not," she replied crisply. "I will tend to this matter at once, Josh. You need not mention this to another soul."

"I will not," Joshua agreed, breathing audibly in relief. "Thank you, Miss Balfour."

Swallowing the lump growing in her windpipe, Emmeline walked slowly toward her father's office where Xavier still remained with Charlton.

"...Greene, Father? Truly? She is worthy of no less than a duke," Emmeline heard her brother growl. "You know as well as I do that Walter Greene has quite the unsavory reputation."

"His reputation is the least of my concerns," Charlton barked. "I will not have you question my decisions in this hotel. When I die, you may run the Balfour Hotel any way you deem fit. Until then—"

"By then it will be too late to save my sister from marriage to a despicable scoundrel!"

Emmeline waited, her heart hammering. She ignored Matthew who stared at her with disapproval as she listened.

"When you are manager of this hotel, Xavier, you will realize that there are many choices to be made, most of which are unpleasant. You and your sister have been fortunate enough to escape the dirt and grime involved with running such an operation but I cannot shield you forever."

"What does that mean, Father?" Xavier snapped. "What has Walter Greene done for you that you owe him your best asset in appreciation?"

Emmeline's heart thudded so loudly, she was shocked the men could not hear it.

"Leave it be, Xavier and mind your sister. If you suspect she is becoming unruly, I expect you to tell me at once."

"I will not spy upon Emmeline."

Xavier has always been my protector.

"You almost ruined everything by telling her of this engagement," Charlton hissed. "If you wish to remain inherited, you will do precisely as you are told."

Xavier scoffed and stormed from the office before Emmeline could make herself scarce. He paused to look at her with regret but moved away again without another word.

"Father?" Emmeline called after a moment. She did not want him to know she had been listening.

"What is it now?" Charlton grumbled.

"This matter is not pertaining to the engagement," she assured him, re-entering the office.

"Do be quick about it, Emmy. I have other matters to attend today, ones which do not include placating your ego."

Emmeline bristled but wisely said nothing to the rebuff.

"I was told that you terminated Mother's abigail. Christiana Compton?"

Her father's head jerked up from his pile of papers and his eyes narrowed into slits.

"What is the meaning of this now?" he growled. Emmeline blinked in surprise at his reaction.

"Did you relieve her for stealing?" Emmeline asked, noting the tight expression on her father's face.

"I do not recall," he retorted, shifting his gaze away, but it was clear to Emmeline that he was being far less than truthful.

"Antoinette claims you did, Father."

"Then she must be correct. What have you to do with this matter?"

The brusque tone was laced with something harder.

Suspicion. He sounds rife with suspicion.

"Father, you do not intermingle with the affairs of the staff. Why did you terminate Christiana personally?"

Charlton grunted and raised his head again, casting Emmeline a stony look.

"Perhaps because she was your mother's abigail. I genuinely do not recall the circumstances, Emmeline. Why are you asking about this? It was months past."

"I would like to speak with Christiana," Emmeline told him flatly. "Yet no one seems to know where she has gone."

"Back home," Charlton replied without hesitation and it gave Emmeline a deeper suspicion.

"How can you be sure?" she asked slowly.

"She wailed about it when she left here, sobbing that she would need to return to...wherever it was she was from."

"Cambridge?" Emmeline asked softly.

"Yes! Yes, that is it. Good riddance, if you ask me. Why would you wish to communicate with riffraff like that? I forbid it. You will not contact that woman."

Emmeline stared at him, her mind whirling.

He is lying to me but why? What has he to do with Christiana's disappearance?

"Is there another matter?" Charlton demanded as he realized that his daughter remained.

"No," she murmured. "That is all. Good day, Father."

With her pulse racing, Emmeline rushed out of the office and made her way toward the staff quarters, her head low.

What became of Christiana Compton? What is Father hiding?

She stopped before Joshua's chambers and rapped gently on the door. There was no response.

"Elias?" she whispered. "Are you in there?"

The door opened in a whoosh, startling her and Elias gaped at her in puzzlement.

"He told you I was here?" he demanded, shocked, but Emmeline shook her head and pushed her way inside, closing the door at her back before they could be noticed. It was midway through the daytime shift but there was still a chance they might be seen.

"It is not how you think," Emmeline assured him. "Joshua only wishes to help you. He told me you were here, but your secret is safe."

Elias eyed her warily and backed toward the bed, sitting on the edge, deep concern etched in his features.

"I mean no harm by being here," he told her. "I will be on my way when I learn where Christiana may have gone."

"You should not have been terminated. Was it Honor who released you?"

He nodded, his lovely, bright eyes fixed on her face in such a way that it made her tingle with warmth.

"Why? For what cause?" she asked, remaining by the door. She knew how inappropriate it was for her to be in the closed room with a male servant. She could only imagine the chaos which would ensue if anyone were to see them sneaking about in such a fashion, but in that moment, Emmeline did not care.

Being proper has earned me a louse of a fiancé and no respect. If I can reunite this man with his wife, perhaps I shan't care about improprieties...

Again, small ripples of unhappiness flowed through her.

He is already married, Emma.

"He learned that Christiana and I...that..." He seemed to have difficulty saying what Emmeline already knew.

"That you are married," she sighed. "He should not have terminated you. I will have him reinstate your position at once."

"I do not think that is wise, Miss Balfour," he told her quietly. "I have the distinct impression that there is much more happening here than I am meant to know."

He sighed and shook his head, staring down at the splintered floor beneath his feet.

"Did you know Christiana when she worked here?"

"Not well," Emmeline confessed regretfully. "She was always pleasant."

"She does not always have her wits about her, but I assure you, Miss Balfour, she is no thief."

"May I ask..." Emmeline bit her lower lip, unsure if she was breaching discretion.

"You may ask me anything."

Emmeline met Elias' steadfast gaze with her own. The mere statement had a profound effect on her and she was once again surprised that a stranger could arouse such emotions in her as Elias had managed in mere hours of knowing him.

What would it be like to spend weeks or months in his presence?

She forced herself not to indulge in such thoughts. Elias was a married man and she was as good as engaged.

Not to mention the fact that we are classes apart.

Queer how those elements seemed unimportant in that moment.

"It is a peculiar arrangement you have with Christiana. Why did you not come to Luton with her for work?" Emmeline asked. "Clearly you would have been hired."

A mirthless smile spread across his lips and a darkness shadowed Elias' features.

"I am afraid that is a tale which is long and sordid," he muttered. "One which I would not offend your ears to explain."

"Did she abandon the martial home?" Emmeline asked before she could consider the crassness of her query, but to her surprise, Elias laughed.

"In a manner of speaking, yes," he replied vaguely. "But ours is not your usual marriage."

"I can see that," Emmeline muttered. "Forgive my intrusive questions. I am merely hoping to help you better in your quest to find her. If she does not wish to be found…"

She trailed off, hoping he understood the implication of her words.

"I can see why you might think such a thing," Elias sighed. "Yet I know Christiana. I am the only person whom she trusts implicitly. She would not vanish without sending word. You must believe me in this matter. Something untoward has happened to her, I am certain of it."

Emmeline did not pretend to understand his faith in his words but she did believe him.

"I will help you find your wife, Elias," she promised him quietly. "I do believe you."

His eyes shone with gratitude and, if she was not mistaken, admiration.

"Thank you, Miss Balfour," he breathed. "I assure you that I will not be here a moment longer than necessary."

She offered him a stiff smile, but her heart was heavy.

When he finds his wife, he will leave and I will remain here with Walter Greene. Which one of us is the poorer?

CHAPTER SIX

Tears streaked her face and she collapsed into his outstretched arms in a heaving sob.

"Good Lord, Christa! What has happened?" Elias choked, pulling his friend to her feet. He looked about the narrow street, expecting to see someone on her trail but there was no one but the usual passersby going about their daily business.

"My life is ruined!" Christiana wailed. "It is over!"

"Hush now," Elias told her worriedly, steering her stumbling form inside. His parents were in the shop and for that, Elias was grateful. He did not wish them to see Christiana in such hysterics. They already had a lowly opinion of his childhood companion and he did not need to fuel their distaste.

"I cannot!" Christiana moaned. "I must leave Peterborough, Elias. I am damned!"

"Lower your voice," Elias told her with soothing exasperation. Her shrill tones could carry easily in house and he did not want the servants to overhear whatever it was this time with Christiana. The scene was commonplace enough, after all, the young woman running to his home with some woe or another and as she had since they were mere children. Elias would simply placate her until she was no longer a sobbing mess.

"I cannot!" she howled. "My life is..."

She buried her face into her hands and shook her dark hair so that the strands fell about her round face in a mess of tangles. She looked as though she had not slept in days.

"Come along," he told her, guiding her into the front room to sit upon the settee as he fetched her a glass of sherry.

Eagerly, Christiana took it with trembling hands, downing it in one smooth gulp before nodding toward it, signaling for another.

My word, Elias thought, gritting his teeth. If I return her home drunk, I will never hear the end of it.

"Perhaps you should tell me what the matter is before I indulge you with another." He sat by her side on the sofa. As she turned toward him, her face was waxen.

"You will loathe me," she moaned. "You will dismiss me as quickly as the townsfolk when you hear of this."

"Christa," he sighed. "I have been your friend since we were wee. I have seen you through some trying affairs and yet I still remain, do I not?"

"This is quite different, Elias. This is..." She sobbed again and Elias produced a handkerchief from his breast pocket for her to dab her eyes.

"I will not know if you do not tell me," he cajoled gently. "Surely you came here because you trust I am your friend."

She looked up at him with glazed eyes, horror below their surface.

"I have sprained my ankle, Elias."

He reeled backward as though she had physically struck him and gasped in shock.

"Christiana!" he rasped. "Are you certain?"

She lowered her gaze and nodded shamefully.

"I am."

Rage replaced the surprise and Elias leapt to his feet, his face growing hot with fury.

"Who is this dastardly urchin?" he yelled, forgetting his desire to keep the conversation quiet. "Tell me who he is and I will see him do right by you!"

"You cannot," Christiana moaned.

"Does he know?" Elias demanded and she shook her head miserably.

"You must tell him, Christa. For all you know, he will marry you well before anyone knows you are with child."

"I cannot tell him," she mumbled and blood pumped through Elias' veins like lava.

"This is not the time to entrench yourself in pity, Christiana. What will you do without a father for the child? You will be ridiculed, condemned."

"You think I do not know that?" she mewled. "I am well aware."

"You give me his name at once. I will see him do right by you!"

"He is gone, Elias. He left town to be with another woman."

"Tarnation!"

She dropped her head again and for the first time remained quiet as tears silently zigzagged down her cheeks.

Slowly, Elias returned to sit at her side and wrap an arm around her shoulders.

"You must not fret now, Christa," he told her with more confidence than he felt. "All will be well."

"What is the meaning of this now?" Rose Compton snapped, stalking into the front room, pulling her gloves from her hands as she glared at the two. "This is inappropriate, Elias. I need not tell you that!"

At his side, Christiana tensed but Elias did not remove his arm of comfort from her shoulders.

She is my friend, he reminded himself. Since childhood. She is the closest I have to a sister and she is in trouble. I cannot turn her away.

"I was leaving, Mrs. Compton," Christiana murmured, wiping the tears from her face as she moved, but Elias rose with her.

"We are happy you are here, Mother," Elias told Rose. "Christa and I have an announcement."

Christiana's face was nearly ashen as she stared at him in disbelief.

"N-no," she gasped but he squeezed her hand gently to reassure her, keeping his eyes fixed upon his mother's annoyed face.

"What announcement would that be?" Rose asked coldly.

"We are getting married. Immediately."

Both women choked and coughed but Elias did not falter.

"You will ruin your life binding yourself to this wench!" Rose howled. "I forbid it!"

"You have no say in the matter, Mother," Elias assured her, casting Christiana a sidelong look. "The matter is done."

"She is with child!" Rose breathed with realization, her hand over her heart as she began to swoon.

"She is with my child," he conceded.

As the door to Joshua's chambers swung inward, Elias opened his eyes, the memory of that fateful day fading yet leaving a melancholy taste to linger.

"You remained!" Joshua cried, appearing very relieved. "I feared that Miss Balfour may not have honored her promise, but of course she did. She is nothing if not honorable."

The younger man smiled warmly at his new friend and Elias righted himself.

"She is many noble things," Elias agreed, thinking about the generous-hearted woman who had left hours earlier after her vow to help him find Christiana.

She does not know me. She has no reason to help me and yet she does not hesitate. She is truly a fine lady.

He had considered that perhaps there was more to her offer, and that maybe she, too, felt the immense connection between them.

Nonsense. She is an heiress to a hotel and to her you are a married, lowly waiter.

"I have a matter to discuss with you," Joshua told him, plopping into the single chair next to the scarred writing desk. "However, I must warn you that it may be something you will not like to know."

"Is it a matter regarding Christiana?"

Joshua nodded, his boyish smile fading slightly but holding.

"It is."

"Then I do not care how unpleasant it may be. What have you learned?"

Joshua leaned forward and met Elias' eyes intently.

"I have been asking the other members of the staff about her. I knew her somewhat, you understand, but I did not fraternize with her outside of the hotel."

"I did not realize that much fraternizing was done outside of the hotel," Elias muttered. Joshua seemed embarrassed.

"Well...ah, in Christiana's case, it seems she did leave with some frequency. More than the others. She had been reprimanded by Antoinette for being late twice in the week which she was terminated, both times were shifts in which she worked the night."

Elias was pensive.

"That was not commonplace for her? To be late?"

"Apparently not. She was known to be dutiful and the guests liked her..."

Joshua stopped speaking and Elias could see that he was attempting to gather his words before he continued.

"Elias, there is gossip that she had a lover."

Wind whooshed out of Elias' lungs and he closed his eyes.

Of course she did. That makes the most sense.

"I am terribly sorry to tell you this," Joshua rushed on, mistaking Elias' reaction for the upset of a husband learning that his wife was unfaithful.

"It would not be the first time," Elias chuckled lightly, opening his eyes and shaking his head. "Tell me more. Who is this man?"

Joshua shrugged.

"Some thought it might be a guest, perhaps one of the noblemen who pass through. Others suspected that it was another member of the staff, but there would be no reason for her to hide that from the other chambermaids. Relations among staff are frowned upon, but if they are kept discrete and do not affect the hotel, management turns the other cheek on the matter. No one knew she was married, Elias. She did not mention it one time."

"She would not," Elias agreed. "I am unsurprised."

"How are you so calm about the matter?" Joshua asked, sounding alarmed. "Even if she was prone to affairs. How could you permit her to come here alone, knowing the kind of woman she is?"

"The tale is complex, Josh," Elias explained. "My only concern is for Christiana's safety, not her behavior."

"You are a queer man, Elias Compton."

"And you, Joshua Milner, are a good friend. Thank you for all you have done thus far. I should not stay here, however. I have been worried all afternoon that you will be caught."

Joshua smiled.

"If you have Miss Balfour as your ally, I feel much more confident in hiding you here. Clearly, we cannot do this for an extended period of time but I will continue to investigate."

"I feel rather useless and ungrateful sitting about while you and Miss Balfour speak to the staff. Surely there must be another way that I can explore the hotel without being detected."

Joshua's smile broadened and he winked conspiratorially.

"As a matter of fact," he tittered. "There happens to be secret compartments all through the hotel, tunnels and old dumb waiter shafts which are unmanned and easily accessed—if one knows where to look."

"And might I venture a guess and say that you are one who might know?" Elias jested.

"Of course!" Joshua laughed. "We will go exploring when the hotel retires for the night. I cannot promise you will find anything, but at least you will not be idle."

"I owe you a debt of gratitude, Josh," Elias told him earnestly. "When I have found Christiana, I will see that you are repaid in kind."

The boy snickered.

"I would be fibbing if I told you that I am not enjoying the excitement. Life about the hotel can get quite mundane. Perhaps I am doing this as much for myself as I am for you."

"I doubt that very much," Elias told him. "But I appreciate it all the same."

"You may thank me by not getting caught," Joshua quipped and Elias nodded, smiling.

"It is a deal, my friend."

CHAPTER SEVEN

The pianoforte played mellifluously throughout the ballroom, a subtle but cheerful rendition.

Haydn, Emmeline realized as she glided through the room, the corners of her rosebud mouth raised in a faux smile. A gracious serenity radiated about her, but it was there by rote rather than design.

I am a perfectly trained house pet, groomed and shiny, paraded about to dazzle the guests as always. I must be witty, but dare not speak too much. I must be articulate, but dare not voice an opinion.

Her gown of pale lavender accentuated her golden-brown eyes, the color flattering against the hypnotic waver of the candles systematically placed about the ever-filling hall.

"You look lovely tonight, Emmy," Xavier told her graciously, extending his arm for her to take. She accepted it eagerly, happy it was her brother who walked beside her and not Walter Greene, who had yet to appear.

"Thank you. You are also quite dashing," she replied graciously although she was not exaggerating. His thick, blonde hair was swept back stylishly, exposing his handsome face and intelligent eyes.

"I must tell you how much I admire your strength," he told her quietly as they nodded at the various guests.

"Strange. I do not feel strong," she confessed in a breath. "I feel as though I am about to float away."

Xavier cast her a sidelong look but they did not slow their gait until he stopped at the buffet and released her arm.

"You will not float away," he promised. "Regardless of what happens, I will always be here. You must know that."

She looked gratefully at him and smiled.

"You are a good brother," she told him.

"Ah, Mr. Xavier, Miss Balfour. What a pleasure." They turned to face the Duke of Workenshire who beamed at them gleefully.

Emmeline curtsied as Xavier bowed and the Duke nodded to them.

"I daresay there is not a finer duo in this room tonight," the Duke announced.

"You are too kind, Your Grace," Emmeline told him demurely.

"I only speak in truths, Miss Balfour. I daresay that after tonight, there will be many a shattered bachelor in Luton."

Emmeline's smile faded quickly and she glanced at Xavier who seemed equally surprised by the Duke's words.

"Your Grace?" she asked.

"Oh, my dear, there is no need to be coy. It is the talk of all of Luton that you will be announcing your engagement tonight. Forgive me for carrying on—I assure you I will act surprised when Mr. Greene declares your betrothal."

Apprehension snaked its way through Emmeline and she looked to her brother as the Duke excused himself.

"Does the entire town know of this?" she snapped in disgust. "Was I truly meant to be the last to learn of Father's plans? Of my own betrothal?"

"I am sorry, Emmy," Xavier said helplessly and she easily read the misery in his face.

It is not Xavier who deserves your anger. It is Father and that wretch, Walter Greene.

"Mother has arrived," Xavier muttered and more tension tightened Emmeline's shoulders. She turned her head to find her mother grinning foolishly as she scanned the room with eyes that failed to focus.

She wore a black dress that was more appropriate for a wake than a lavish gala.

"Good heavens, what is she wearing?" Emmeline muttered more to herself than Xavier but her brother was equally displeased.

"I will not play governess to her tonight," he vowed, but Emmeline knew that was precisely what he would do. Charlton would be preoccupied with his own matters, ignoring his wife at best, demeaning her at worst. It would be Xavier's duty to ensure that all ran smoothly, particularly when Anne already had her lips pressed to a goblet of champagne.

"Lord, help us," Xavier mumbled, hurrying toward his mother's side. Sighing, Emmeline looked away, her eyes resting on Joshua who circulated the party with a silver tray of crystal-stemmed glasses.

She had not seen him nor Elias since the previous day, the preparations for the gala overtaking her morning and afternoon. Nevertheless, she had been unable to stop thinking about them, despite her own worries.

I must speak to Joshua alone. Perhaps there is some information on where Christiana has gone.

She nodded to Lord Edmund and Lady Chisholm as they approached, but quickly ducked away from the crowd, hoping to catch Joshua's attention. He was far too consumed with his work to notice her at first.

Perhaps I could slip away to his quarters and see Elias myself, she thought. The notion tantalized her far more than it should have. If she disappeared from the party, she would undoubtedly be missed and someone might come looking for her.

But all the staff is here tonight. I would barely be seen if I go.

Indecisively, she remained in place.

What would I tell him if I do go to him? There is no reason for me to visit him. I have no news on his...wife.

She continued to struggle with the concept of Elias being married.

"Miss Balfour, would you care for champagne?"

Joshua. Her body heaved with relief.

"Thank you, Josh," she murmured, accepting a goblet from the tray. "I was hoping to speak with you alone."

"I fear this is not the best time, Miss."

"I concur," she agreed hurriedly, feeling foolish that she had suggested it at all. "Do answer me this—is all well with our mutual friend?"

Joshua swallowed a smile and darted his eyes downward.

"I daresay all is well. He is nearer than you might think," Joshua said, his eyes pointedly fixing behind her on the wall.

She turned her head and followed his gaze in confusion.

"I do not understand."

"Lower, Miss Balfour. The grate."

Her eyes dropped and she gasped, almost losing hold of her glass when she saw hints of a dashing face and a set of familiar, piercing eyes peering up at them. Elias grinned from his hiding place, pressing his index finger to his lips.

"My word..." Emmeline muttered, her face flushing. "I have not used those passages since I was a child."

Joshua tittered.

"I remember. We found them together."

She nodded but her eyes were still trained on Elias, her skin prickling as he held her gaze.

"Miss Balfour," Joshua whispered. "I believe you will be needed in a moment."

"How is that?"

Joshua did not answer but suddenly, a voice boomed across the room as the music died.

"Ladies and gentlemen," Charlton called from the head of the room. "May I have your attention please?"

The din in the ballroom quieted and all guests focused on the proprietor as he scanned the faces of the crowd.

"I would like to thank you all for joining us at our annual winter gala," he began, his eyes found and rested on Emmeline sending a spark of frightened nervousness shooting through her.

"Tonight is a special occasion, not only because we are entrenched in dapper lords and fine ladies," he continued to a round of appreciative laughter. "But also because the Balfours have a special announcement this fine evening."

Charlton tore his eyes away from Emmeline as Walter Greene suddenly appeared beside him. The portly man could not manage a smile for the crowd and instead scowled defiantly as if he had no interest in being there.

"Many of you know Mr. Walter Greene. His business is renowned in Luton and abound."

There was a shift in the atmosphere, a slight murmur erupting in the group and Emmeline could plainly see the disdain many of the attendees felt toward the businessman.

"This is why it is my great honor to announce that Mr. Greene will be joining the Balfour family as my daughter's husband."

Charlton smiled broadly and gestured for Emmeline to join them but her feet felt like lead sinking into the polished floor.

"Miss Balfour," Joshua breathed. "They are waiting on you."

She gulped back the stone lodged in her throat and propelled herself forward but the forced smile would not come, no matter how she tried to muster it.

You must not make a scene, she warned herself and as the thought crossed her mind. She sought out her mother among the guests who were doing their best to look congratulatory.

Anne smirked at Emmeline but there was an unmistakable sorrow in the older woman's eyes.

"Emmeline," Charlton told her, grasping her gloved hand in his own white clad fingers. "You are my only daughter and I have dreamed of the day that you will wed a fine gentleman."

Emmeline lowered her gaze, feeling the burn of Walter Greene's beady eyes upon her.

"Mr. Greene, I welcome you to our family with open arms," Charlton cried and Emmeline could hear the faux note of geniality in his words. "Would you care to say anything?"

He turned to Walter but to everyone's surprise, Walter only grunted.

"I will save my speech for the wedding," he grumbled.

"A man of few words, our Mr. Greene," Charlton laughed and the crowd joined him, an air of discomfort hanging over the party. "Let us not embarrass him further. We shall continue the festivities, shan't we?"

Walter shuffled away with another grunt and Emmeline found herself staring after him in disbelief.

"Father," she breathed, reaching out for Charlton. "He does not seem to be keen on this marriage."

Charlton glared at her.

"Do not speak nonsense, Emmeline. Every bachelor in Luton deigns to marry you."

"But Father—"

"I will not hear another word on this subject, are we clear?" Charlton hissed, his face contorting in fury. "If you insist on being petulant, I will make arrangements for you until the wedding."

Arrangements? She thought, stunned, but she did not voice her question aloud. She was certain she would not enjoy the answer.

"When will the wedding take place, Father?" she asked instead and Charlton visibly relaxed slightly as he studied her eyes for signs of trouble.

"Soon," he told her. "There is no need for a long engagement."

The response tied knots of dread in Emmeline's stomach and she turned from her father whose attention had already been diverted elsewhere.

Suddenly remembering the bronzed grate where she knew Elias had been hiding, her heart raced.

Does it much matter to him that I am engaged now? She wondered, slowly making her way back to where she had last seen him. Something in her longed to see his bright eyes staring out at her, but as she reclaimed her vantage point near the wall, Elias was no longer visible behind the vent cover.

Her chest felt heavy as she wilted against the wall. Never had she felt so alone or confused.

I am to marry a man I do not like, let alone love, and my family does not care.

She did not wish to feel pity for herself but the melancholy was nearly overwhelming.

Many women have married men like Walter Greene and led perfectly successful lives, she reasoned rationally, but it did little to ease her sadness. She turned away from the wall but as she did, she noticed a small scrap of paper folded over the bottom of the grate, the edge just barely visible. Her brow furrowed, Emmeline leaned down to pick it up, certain that it had not been there earlier.

She opened it up, looking about for some clue as to how it may have gotten there.

Turret rooftop. 9 o'clock.

No sooner did she read the words than the grandfather clocks begin to chime the hour of nine.

She looked about, unsure for whom the message was meant, but in her heart, she felt that it was for her and the writer, she was certain, was none other than Elias Compton.

There is only one way to know for sure, she thought, glancing furtively about as though going to the roof was a sin in itself.

There is no sin, she told herself as she slipped out of the ballroom, amidst the well-wishers who surrounded her. *It only feels like one.*

Yet she had no reservations about stealing away to see if it truly was she that Elias expected to meet on the roof.

CHAPTER EIGHT

A light mist rained down upon the open turret and Elias rubbed his bare hands against his arms, wishing he had thought to find a coat before venturing outside but he heard the toll of church bells indicating the hour of nine. It was too late to sneak back inside.

If she comes at all. She may not. She may not have even seen my note.

Suddenly, Elias felt very foolish.

"Elias?"

He whirled at the sound of Emmeline's voice and exhaled with relief as she stole through the shadows toward him.

"You came," he breathed. "I was unsure if you would—"

"Of course I came," she replied quietly, carefully closing the distance between them. She shivered slightly and again, Elias cursed himself for not having a coat for her.

"Forgive the covert surroundings. I feared that I would encounter Mrs. Baxter or Mr. Wesley with all the fuss."

"No," Emmeline replied softly. "Despite the cold, I relish the quiet."

"I suspected as much."

She peered at him quizzically.

"Why have you called me here?"

THE HEIRESS'S SECRET LOVE

Because I am a fool, he wanted to say, but he did not.

"I thought you could use an escape for a short time," he said instead. "Forgive me for being presumptuous."

"Not at all," she said softly. "You were quite right. Were my sentiments that obvious?"

"Even from the confines of a grate," he laughed but he knew the matter was not one for jesting. He cleared his throat and looked away.

"Forgive me, Miss Balfour. I should be congratulating you on your betrothal."

"Thank you." Her response was stiff.

"Have you known Mr. Greene long?" Elias knew he was grasping at conversation and again, he considered that he had acted improperly by boldly inviting her to such a private interview.

"I do not know Mr. Greene at all but to say he is an associate of my father's."

"Oh…I-I see."

An uncomfortable silence ensued and they glanced at one another nervously.

"Did you know Christiana before you married her?"

Elias sighed.

"We were childhood friends."

"How charming," Emmaline offered, yet she did not look pleased. "You had always known you would wed then."

Elias scoffed before he could stop himself and shook his head.

"Hardly. She is like a sister to me."

His head jerked up and he met her stunned gaze, his ears heating amidst the cold.

"I-it is a complex matter," he mumbled, but he felt he owed her more than his usual response.

She has gone out of her way to help me find Christiana. I should be frank with her. Christiana need not know I spoke out of school.

"Christa has always been difficult, even when she was very young. She is the last of six children and I suspect that she was very much lost in the fold which is why she looked for affirmation anywhere she could find it—and with anyone."

He gritted his teeth together, less from the chill in the air and more because he realized he had never spoken the story aloud before.

"You need not explain it to me," Emmeline told him gently. "Your personal affairs are your own."

"If you'll permit me, I'd like you to know," Elias insisted. "It is simply not a tale I have spoken of outside of my own head."

She did not say a word and instead waited for him to finish the story he had started.

"She was unruly, never listening, never acting properly and soon she had earned a reputation for herself in Peterborough, one which was not befitting of such a sweet girl. You must understand, Miss Balfour, Christa was never cruel or malicious, merely wayward."

"I have nothing but fond memories of her," Emmeline conceded.

"She came to me one day, three years ago, sobbing. She was with child and the father had run off with another woman."

Emmeline gasped, already sensing what he was about to say next.

"My family was in decent standing in Peterborough and hers could not withstand more shame brought upon them so I took it upon myself to marry her. I wanted to save her, but Christa, she has no desire to be saved."

"My word...you are a saint, Elias."

"I am a fool," he snapped back. "She lost the child or so she claimed. I have no way of knowing if ever there truly was a child. I was left married to an unsound woman who resented me for the union. She came and went as she pleased. She had lovers, blatantly and without shame. My parents were furious with the way she besmirched our good name. But we were wed and what else was I to do? In the end, she always came home, crying, when something went awry. She knows I care about her, the way a brother cares for a sister, and she knows I am the safest place for her to be."

"That is a terrible burden for you to carry upon yourself," Emmeline told him quietly.

"When she came here, I was relieved. She wrote me and I knew she was alive and whatever debauchery she was getting involved in, it did not affect the Compton name in Peterborough. I thought...I hoped that she would change, grow into a woman and stop being the spoiled child she had always been. And then, she abruptly stopped writing. I know in my heart that she is unsafe somewhere, Miss Balfour and I must find her."

Emmeline nodded slowly and the mist of rain glittered in her golden hair like diamond droplets.

"We will find her," she promised. "At any cost. Thank you for telling me this, Elias. I feel as though I know you better now."

"I must swear you to secrecy," Elias told her. "If Christiana were to know I told, she would feel betrayed."

"Elias, I have not a soul to tell if I wished to," she said and the sadness in her voice was nearly tangible.

"How can that be, Miss Balfour? You are surrounded by people, your family, the servants—"

"And none of them knows me in the least," she interjected. "I am not alone and yet I am lonely."

"I would like to be your friend, Miss Balfour."

She smiled at him wryly.

"My friends call me Emmy."

"Emmy," he said, trying the name on his tongue. "I daresay, I have not known one Emmeline in my life."

"Is that a fact?" she laughed.

"It is. I would not lie to you."

Her eyes locked on his and her lips quavered slightly.

"I believe that," she whispered. "I cannot say why but I feel as though I have known you longer than merely a few days. Is that strange?"

"Not to me. I feel precisely the same."

She cocked her head slightly sideways and studied him.

"You mean to tell me that you are not merely a waiter then?"

Elias laughed. "I have been around enough waiters to know how they operate. I did not think it would be very difficult to fabricate the experience."

"Yet you did not make it through a single shift!" Emmeline teased and Elias laughed.

"Indeed," he replied. "I suppose I will be forced to do better in the future."

"Why did you not simply take a room at the hotel? This was a rather elaborate scheme, becoming part of the staff."

"I considered it, but I felt I would look suspicious questioning the servants as a guest. It is a moot issue now. I have barely learned anything about Christa's whereabouts in the past two days except to know that she has taken yet another lover."

"Here? At the hotel?" Emmeline asked, aghast.

"I am unsure. With the party, it was impossible to gather more information but Joshua assures me he will continue to investigate on my behalf. I have been learning the hotel but she has been gone for so long, I cannot expect to find a trace of her here."

Emmeline was silent but Elias could see her eyes twitching as though her mind raced behind them.

"Emmeline?" he asked tentatively, not sure if she was listening any longer. "Are you well?"

"There are secrets in this hotel," she murmured and Elias nodded.

"There are secrets everywhere," he agreed. "In such a lavish inn with exclusive guests, I am hardly shocked to know there are whispers in dark corners."

"Indeed..."

Emmeline refocussed her gaze upon him and smiled warmly.

"I hope you will not think me rude, Elias, but it is getting quite cold and damp out here and I fear it is only a matter of time before my family comes in search of me."

"I imagine they will question why you are wet," Elias chuckled. "Forgive me, Emmeline. You have most graciously entertained my whimsy."

"No, you have been most gracious providing me with this escape and with your friendship. I cannot tell you how much it means to me."

They shared a smile and Emmeline gathered her skirts to return to the turret stairs.

"Emmy..."

She glanced over her shoulder at him and Elias felt his heart stop beating for a moment. He was certain he had never seen such radiance, her glimmering strands of hair silhouetted by the blackened sky, her glowing amber eyes warming him even from the distance between them.

"Yes?"

"You look very beautiful tonight."

Her blush was apparent even in the darkness and she hung her head demurely.

"Thank you, Elias."

She vanished then and Elias exhaled in a torrent of wind, his body suddenly feeling leagues lighter as though he had removed weights from his shoulders.

How long has it been since I have spoken to someone the way I have Joshua and Emmeline these past days? When Christa is around, we squabble and when she is gone, I am alone. How long has it been since I have had a friend?

It was a daunting thought, one he had not considered until that moment. He had spent so much time chasing Christiana and ensuring her safety, he had forgotten to care for himself.

"No, Emmy," he sighed to no one but the blowing wind around him. "Thank you."

For even though there can never be anything between us, you have given me much.

CHAPTER NINE

The morning following the gala, Emmeline rose very early and dressed quickly without the assistance of her abigail. She wished to make herself as scarce as possible before the household arose and noticed her missing, but she was not early enough.

The first soul she encountered was her father in the hallway of the fifth floor. He seemed as startled to see her as she did him.

"Emmy? What are you doing about?" Charlton asked, glancing behind him as though he expected someone else to join them in the corridor.

"Oh...I..." Emmeline thought quickly. "I suppose the excitement of last evening has traveled through to this morrow."

He nodded curtly but she got the distinct impression that he was not paying any particular mind to her excuse.

"Of course. I must be on my way," he told her, moving through. Emmeline watched him turn the corner toward the staircase. She had been heading toward the service stairs to find Elias, but something inherent caused her to change her mind and follow her father.

Is he acting suspicious or do I merely see that in everyone now?

She decided to find out where it was Charlton headed at that hour.

She knew her father's schedule well enough to know that he did not often rise before dawn.

Unless he has business matters to attend to, she thought, stealthily gliding after him. Emmeline was careful to ensure that she was not seen but there were few people who might catch glimpse of her. Regardless, she took special care to be cautious.

Through the center staircase, Charlton moved, barely looking about and Emmeline wondered if she was acting foolishly by chasing after him.

He certainly does not seem perturbed. Perhaps there is no reason for my suspicion.

Yet, she continued on and when she reached the lobby, she remained hidden in the shadows. The concierge was not at his posting but Walter Greene stood at the entry desk, seeming impatient.

"What an ungodly hour to meet," her betrothed snapped at her father. "Could we not have done this another time?"

"I explained already that this is for discretion's sake," Charlton sighed, ushering Walter toward his office. His head twisted around and Emmeline ducked lower against the bannister, hoping her blonde crown did not show over the intricate railing. She exhaled with relief when the men disappeared inside the office, closing the door.

I must find out what they are discussing in there, Emmeline thought, rising to hurry toward the closed room. She had the distinct sense that she was the topic of their conversation.

With another furtive look around, she pressed herself between the wall and the closed door, her eyes trained outward lest anyone chance upon her spying on the pair. Through the thick door, their voices were muffled but audible.

"...than later, Balfour. I do not wish to wait a minute longer than necessary for my money," Walter growled. "I have already extended you enough courtesy in this matter."

"And I have delivered all that I have promised thus far, have I not?"

"Not all."

"These matters take time, Walter. I cannot simply sign away the holdings without the benefit of marriage. My son will undoubtedly ask questions—"

"These are not my concerns. You will reign in your boy as necessary."

"I understand your impatience, Walter, truly I do, but you must exercise resolve for only a few more weeks until the wedding. A portion of the hotel will be signed to you as Emmeline's dowry and you will be part owner of the Balfour as I have vowed."

"I will expect a bigger percentage in that case," Walter told him and there was a gasp of shock.

"That was not our agreement," her father muttered. "You will hold thirty percent, not a fraction more."

"If I am to wait weeks, I will expect to be recompensed for it," Walter insisted.

"And what of the other matter I attended?" Charlton bit back sharply. "If I had not seen to your mishap with the chambermaid—"

"No one asked you to tend to that!"

Gooseflesh erupted over Emmeline's skin and she drew back, her hand on her heart as if to still it from beating clear out of her chest.

What chambermaid? Are they speaking of Christiana?

She thought of how her father had acted when she had confronted him with Christiana's dismissal and a sliver of terror made her shiver.

What have they done to her and why?

It took every iota of control in her body not to burst through the door and demand answers, her only reason stemming from the fear growing in her gut.

"What I did, I did for the good of this hotel," Charlton muttered in a tone so low, Emmeline was forced to strain her ears. "But I will not have you extort me when I know—"

"You know nothing for certain!" Walter interjected. The fury in his tone was nearly tangible and Emmeline's heart raced.

"I know enough," Charlton retorted. "You will maintain your silence and we will go forth with the wedding in a few weeks, but I will not give you more than we have already discussed."

"You are hardly in a position to make demands of me, Balfour. I have saved your hotel from certain ruination. It is not too late for me to recant on my decision."

"And it will not be too late for me to make your true character known, either," Charlton snapped.

"Not without detriment to your own character," Walter countered.

"Must we go in endless circles with these threats all day? We have an understanding, one which will benefit us both. Why are you determined to upset the apple cart now?"

"Is it not obvious, Balfour? I do not trust you."

"The feeling is more than mutual, Walter and yet I have given you less of a reason than you—"

"Miss Balfour, are you well?"

Emmeline yelped and whirled, shocked and appalled at being caught listening. Honor stood, his face twisted in worry as he stared at her, but she shook her head vehemently, pressing her finger to her lips as she moved away from the door, lest her father and Walter Greene hear them outside.

"No," she whispered urgently. "Honor, please, I am begging you as a friend to forget what you have seen here."

Uncertainty clouded the maître d's eyes and his gaze darted toward the office.

"Miss Balfour, I-I do not know what to say," he mumbled, his complexion paling dramatically.

"Then say nothing at all, Honor," she told him firmly. "I was never here."

She hurried away from his confused stare but she could still feel him watching her well after she stole toward the servant's quarters, her pulse erratic as she tried to make sense of what she had heard in the office.

They are both involved in something terrible but what?

It was evident that her father had come into Walter Greene's debt.

And I am a repayment of said debt, I assume. My dowry includes shares in this hotel. I was correct. Walter Greene has no interest in marrying me, only in ownership of this hotel.

It was troubling that her father was so quick to sell her off to a man who was brutish and had not shown the least bit of warmth toward her, but more than that, there was something sinister about the impending marriage.

They were discussing Christiana Compton, of that I am certain. I must tell Elias what I heard, even if it makes little sense.

The staff had risen by now, but Emmeline paid them no mind as she made her way toward Joshua's room. With trembling hands, she rapped gently on the door, unsure if Joshua was scheduled for day or night shift that day. She had been too distracted to check the roster.

"Miss Balfour," Joshua breathed, his hair dishevelled from sleep as he opened the door. "I-I was not expecting you."

"Is Elias here?" she asked in a low voice, peering over his shoulder but Joshua shook his head.

"He left in the night," he explained. "He felt useless sitting about and he went into Luton to see if anyone had seen Christiana."

"Ballocks," Emmeline cursed and Joshua sniggered, covering his hand with his mouth. Embarrassed, she looked away.

"Forgive my crassness," she mumbled. "Please, send for me when he returns. I have a terrible suspicion…"

She stopped speaking, unsure if she should continue to talk so freely.

"Please, Josh, send for me upon his return."

"Yes, Miss Balfour."

The door closed and she stood, debating what to do next.

Antoinette, she realized. *Antoinette knows more than she has said.*

———

Emmeline located the head housekeeper on the fifth floor. She balked when she saw what the housekeeper was tasked with.

"Do be careful, Cora!" Antoinette snapped as the chambermaid huffed along with a huge trunk in her hands. "Mr. Greene will be displeased to find his items in disarray."

"W-what is the meaning of this?" Emmeline demanded, looking at the half dozen servants filling the room adjacent to hers.

Antoinette eyed her warily.

"Your fiancé has taken a suite with the family now," she explained and Emmeline paled at the idea.

"Now? Already?" she choked, although she was not sure why she was surprised. The discussion she had heard that morning certainly indicated that matters would be moving along at a much greater speed than Emmeline could stop.

"Of course," Antoinette told her crisply. "In a few weeks, you will be sharing a suite, will you not?"

I will not think about that, Emmeline told herself firmly.

"May I have a moment with you, Antoinette?"

"Now?"

"Yes," Emmeline said urgently. "It is important."

Begrudgingly, Antoinette nodded and followed Emmeline into her chambers where the younger woman closed the door quietly.

"Forgive my bluntness, Miss Emmeline but there is much work to be done today. What is the matter?"

"I want the truth," Emmeline replied shortly. "In its entirety."

Antoinette seemed perplexed.

"Miss?"

"About Christiana Compton. What became of her truly. I have heard rumors that she had a lover here in the hotel. Is that a fact? Is that why she was terminated?"

Antoinette tensed visibly and she quickly darted her eyes away.

"I would not know about the private affairs of the servants," she said but Emmeline could hear the lie in her voice.

"Antoinette, I know better than anyone how you involve yourself in the comings and goings of the staff. I insist you tell me what you know about her."

"And if I tell you I know nothing?"

"I will tell you that I do not believe you."

The woman met her eyes and Emmeline could see the housekeeper's resolve fading as she held her gaze.

"Is this about her husband arriving here?" Antoinette asked.

"You heard about that?"

"As you said, Miss Emmeline, there is little which happens here that I do not know. Albeit, I did not know Miss Compton was married. She made no mention of it when she applied to work here or we would not have hired her, I assure you. A married woman leaving her husband could not reflect well on the hotel."

"Never mind that now," Emmeline told her. "What happened when she arrived. Did she take a lover?"

Antoinette sighed deeply and pursed her lips together.

"Miss, we do not condone affairs of the heart among the servants but we cannot stop it from occurring," Antoinette muttered.

"I am not faulting anyone, Antoinette. I only wish to know what happened to Christiana. She has disappeared. Her safety is my only concern."

To her surprise, Antoinette scoffed.

"If she has disappeared, I assure you, it was of her own accord."

"You said she was relieved of her duties due to theft but that is not true, is it?" Emmeline pressed. "She was terminated because of this love affair."

"I told you, Miss Emmeline, your father was the one who asked her to leave."

"You know more than that!" Emmeline exploded, her patience falling short as she detected the evasiveness in Antoinette's tone. "You must tell me what you know!"

The housekeeper raised her head and studied Emmeline pensively.

"Why does it matter to you so much, Miss Emmeline? You did not know Christiana."

"Does that matter? She was a servant here and therefore a part of the hotel."

"Is that all?"

Emmeline was sure she did not like Antoinette's tone.

"I have no idea what you are insinuating but if I can help a man find his wife, why does it matter?"

Shock filled Antoinette's face.

"Elias Compton is still in Luton?" she demanded and Emmeline felt the blood slowly drain from her own face.

"I-I am unsure," she mumbled.

Are we having two very different conversations?

"Dear Lord," Antoinette breathed. "He should leave at once. Nothing good will come of him remaining here."

Alarm flowed freely through Emmeline's body.

"How do you mean?" Emmeline demanded, her eyes wide. "Why?"

Antoinette hung her head and shook it warily.

"I cannot say any more, Miss Emmeline. Forgive me."

She turned to rush away but Emmeline would not let her leave, not when she felt the truth was so close to her ears.

"Antoinette, if Elias in danger and something happens to him because of your silence, I will never forgive you!"

The woman turned to look at her in surprise.

"I did not know you had become so close to Mr. Compton," she murmured.

"That is hardly your concern," Emmeline told her boldly although her heart was thudding loudly. "You will tell me all you know."

"You will not leave this be, will you?"

"I will not," Emmeline agreed. "If I must question every member of the staff personally, I will do so."

"If you do that, you will find answers which you will not like."

"I would rather the truth. Has something untoward become of Christiana Compton?"

Antoinette exhaled in a whoosh of air.

"I do not know for certain," she muttered and Emmeline looked to her skeptically.

"Where is she?"

"I sincerely do not know," Antoinette insisted.

"You must do better than that, Antoinette."

"I will tell you what I know, Miss Emmeline but again, you cannot unhear what I know."

"It is a risk I am willing to take."

"We shall see."

Antoinette spun back around, her face pinched and unhappy.

"You may wish to sit, Miss Emmeline. I fear what I have to say will take your breath away."

CHAPTER TEN

The Sweetwater Inn was a quaint tavern on the edge of Luton and despite the early hour of the morning, the proprietor ushered Elias inside, eyeing him with curiosity.

"You do not hail from these parts, do you lad?" the pudgy owner asked, slapping a pint of ale before him. "I would recognize a dashing face like yours, I daresay."

His name was Charlie Blossom and he boasted his open policy for any weary traveler in Luton. The belly-cheat which covered his fat stomach was already filthy as though Charlie had not bothered with the washing of it for many moons, but Elias had matters with which to concern himself other than the man's articles.

"I have come to Luton in search of someone," Elias told him accepting the beverage gratefully. "She worked at the hotel for a time and now she has gone amiss."

"Ah, benish cove you are, seeking a lass who does not wish to be found," the man tittered, leaning across the countertop. "Seen lots of them come and go myself, chambermaids and the lot."

Elias decided not to enlighten the man that the woman he sought was his wife. It would only lead to more questions and it was answers Elias wanted, not queries.

"Do you recall a dark-haired girl with eyes of blue? Comely and plump?"

The proprietor snickered.

"Lad, half of them are blonde, the others are dark. I could not tell you one from the next."

"Her name is Christiana," Elias sighed although he could see that the man did not pay much mind to the names of the women who might have filtered through. It had been Elias' thought that the tavern would be as good a place as any to look for Christiana, knowing her propensity to seek out trouble.

"Christa, you mean?"

Elias' head jerked upward.

"Yes!" he replied eagerly. "You know of her?"

Charlie howled.

"My word," he choked. "I daresay everyone knows of her, lad. She is quite a lass, that one."

He winked leeringly at Elias.

"I might add that you are wasting your time if you hope to court such a woman. She has many admirers and hesitates to smile upon none."

Elias stifled a groan of resignation.

He certainly knows Christiana.

Still, Elias was hopeful. Finding someone outside of the hotel who knew her was certainly more promising than uncovering the truth inside the Balfour household.

"When did you last see her?" Elias asked. "Has it been recent?"

Charlie frowned, his mouth making a moue as he considered the question.

"Maybe a week? No more than a fortnight to be sure."

Elias jumped to his feet, leaning across the bar and stunning Charlie as he reached for him.

"Here? In this very public house?" he gasped. Charlie stepped back, glancing at Elias' face warily.

"Where else? Clearly you can see I am not a man to attend the Balfour galas."

"Was she alone? Where does she stay? Is she well?"

The questions flew from his mouth in a torrent but suddenly Charlie seemed much less amiable.

"What is your business with the lass?" the owner demanded, folding his arms over his chest. "I daresay her beau will have something to say if you go looking for her."

"Her beau?" Elias steeled himself from lurching clear across to shake the words from Charlie's lips.

"Indeed. He works at the hotel also."

"A name, Mr. Blossom. I need a name!"

"I do not care for your tone, sir," Charlie barked back, a blank expression falling over his face. "And I do not owe you a response. You may finish your ale and leave."

"I will not leave until you have given me some answers!" Elias retorted but he did reclaim his seat, willing his anger to subside. "I must know with whom she was."

"I cannot recall."

Elias groaned aloud, knowing he had lost his opportunity to learn anything in his haste.

"Please, Mr. Blossom. I wish only to ensure she is well," he pleaded. "The name of her beau will suffice."

"You could go to the hotel and ask yourself," Charlie recommended crisply, turning toward his stock and pretending to busy himself. It was clear he would be of no further help to Elias.

"Mr. Blossom," he tried again. "You are certain it was as recent as a fortnight that you last saw Christiana?"

"I said as much, did I not?" Charlie snapped back. "You need not ask me again."

That is something, Elias told himself calmly. *She is about Luton but simply does not wish to be found.*

A small part of him told Elias that the answer should have been enough, that he should return to Peterborough and wait for word or for his wife's return now that he knew she was safe.

But do I know that she is safe? Why has she not sent word to me? There is nothing in this world which she could not tell me. Is she being kept against her will?

Charlie's sighting had only created more doubt in Elias and he shook his head, rising from his stool, his pint almost untouched.

"Mr. Blossom," he called but the owner did not turn. He did grunt to acknowledge he had heard Elias.

"If Christiana were to return, would you give her a message for me?"

Slowly, Charlie moved his head to look at Elias over his shoulder.

"Out with it, then."

"Tell her that her husband is in Luton and I am very concerned for her."

Charlie's mouth gaped open and he shuffled toward the counter.

"Crikey, are you truly her husband?"

"I am, Mr. Blossom. Elias Compton."

"That strumpet ran off on you then?" he growled. Defensiveness fused through Elias' bones.

"You must not speak that way of my wife," he snapped and Charlie had the good decency to appear contrite.

"I will pass along the message for you, Mr. Compton but you haven't much to be concerned about. She is well, I promise you as much."

Elias believed him but it was not enough. He needed to see Christiana for himself.

"It would be most useful if you could recall the name of her beau," Elias told him gently. "Or anything about the man at all."

Charlie made a face which told Elias he did not wish to speak out of turn.

"I do not wish to cause problems," Charlie muttered and Elias shook his head quickly.

"Whatever you tell me, Mr. Blossom, I assure you will remain between us. I need not mention your name."

Charlie nodded, apparently convinced by the plaintive look on Elias' face.

"I have a name for you, Mr. Compton but before I say it aloud, I would like to say that I do not believe he knew of her treachery either. He is a good man, not inaptly named."

Elias nodded.

"I fault no one in this matter," he assured Charlie. "There will be no scene made nor blame administered. I only wish to see my wife with my own eyes."

"You are a true gentleman, Mr. Compton. I would not know many men to handle this with such decorum."

"His name, Mr. Blossom, if you please?"

Charlie bobbed his head slowly.

"Of course. His name is Honor. Honor Wesley. He is the maître d' at the Balfour Hotel."

————

There were far too many people milling about for Elias simply to re-enter the building, despite his inherent desire to storm through the service doors and confront Honor directly.

You must not bring attention to yourself. It endangers both Joshua and Emmeline if you are caught.

It was also not in his nature to create a scene, but his blood was boiling as he realized that Honor had known all along where to find Christiana.

That was why he was so eager to be rid of me. He thought I would take her home. He might still be right.

Elias knew he could not force Christiana to return, for even if he managed to drag her back to Peterborough, she would only run off again. Short of locking her away, there was nothing he could do to control the unruly woman he had so foolishly married.

What if she stays here forever? He wondered as he paced along the property line in the cold, waiting for the sun to set so that he might steal his way back inside. *I could return home and forget she existed but at what cost? I could never marry and have a family. What a life I have chosen for myself, all to keep a selfish girl from scorn and ridicule. She could not even be bothered to tell me she is safe.*

Anger towards Christiana coursed through his veins for the first time since he had married her, as if the past three years had been a trance which he had accepted and from which he had only just awoken.

Nothing has changed. She is the same woman you married. You knew how she would be. Why are you so furious now?

The answer was simple. Until he had come to Luton, Elias had never known he could feel so intimately about someone the way he did Emmeline Balfour. He had resigned himself to his life with Christiana, never knowing how love felt.

Now that I understand what it is to feel connected to another, it is too late to understand it, to pursue it.

A weaker man might have justified his feelings and acted upon them with the knowledge that Christiana had never hesitated to commit adultery.

Yet Elias was not such a man, nor would he turn Emmeline into a besmirched woman.

"Elias! My goodness, I thought it was you out here!"

Emmeline rushed toward him, her cheeks flushed with pink as she drew near.

"I have been waiting for you to return all day! Where have you been?" she gasped, abruptly stopping before him. Excitement and worry filled her eyes and Elias was again struck by her breathtaking beauty, her fair coloring against the black of her articles.

"I have word on Christiana," he told her, wrenching his eyes away from the creamy skin of her swelling bosom which barely peeked through the thick of her wool cloak.

"As do I!" Emmeline gushed, reaching out a black gloved hand toward him. She had not meant to touch him but when she did, he instantly felt a spark of electricity between them which warmed him from toes to nose.

Elias swallowed and met her gaze, seeing that she, too, had felt the surge of energy and she offered him a shy smile, though her eyes remained shadowed.

"You know then," Elias said quickly. "Who her lover is?"

Emmeline nodded and in unison, they each spoke a name.

"Honor Wesley," Elias muttered.

"Walter Greene," Emmeline answered simultaneously.

They gaped at one another.

"What?" they chorused. "Are you certain?"

Unexpectedly they laughed, although they both knew it was hardly a comical matter, but Elias continued quickly.

"I went to a tavern in town. The barkeep insisted that he saw her in Mr. Wesley's company not a fortnight past. What makes you say that it is your fiancé?"

"Antoinette told me as much. My father offered her a great deal of money to leave when he learned of it."

"And yet she remained in town?" Elias mused. "Not that anything Christa does shocks me much. It is possible she has two lovers, maybe even more."

"You poor man," Emmeline murmured, the compassion in her eyes shining through. "How do you cope knowing what she does?"

Elias shook his head indifferently, but inside he was seething with humiliation, the unfairness of the situation overwhelming him.

"If what you say is true, Emmeline, your betrothed is not much better."

She grimaced but shook her head as if to refocus her thoughts.

"That is a matter for another time, Elias," Emmeline told him, leaning closer. "The tale is worse than you could imagine."

"Oh, I doubt that it could be much worse," Elias replied, inhaling the scent of her hair as she drew closer. He hoped that he would forever cling to the memory of her nearness.

"Then I fear you are mistaken."

Elias peered at her, his jaw locking in anticipation.

"What is it?" he muttered. "Where is she now?"

"That I do not know," she said quietly. "What I am about to tell you will be difficult to hear, Elias."

"Tell me," he urged. "I must know."

She bit on her lip and stared at him with sympathetic eyes.

"If what Antoinette has told me is true, Christiana is with child."

CHAPTER ELEVEN

"Wait!" Emmeline cried out as Elias rushed past her toward the hotel. "Elias, you must not—"

Her pleas fell on deaf ears for he was already entering through the service doors. There was nothing she could do but hurry after him, cursing herself for having spoken so boldly.

He cannot confront Walter Greene. The man is far too dangerous. If he and my father learn that Elias is looking into them...

She could not fathom what they might do to protect their investments and interests.

Emmeline flew after Elias, looking about in desperation when she entered but she could not immediately see where he had gone.

"Cora!" she called to the chambermaid shuffling through the kitchen. "Where is Honor?"

Cora blinked and shrugged but Emmeline was already on the move, racing toward the dining room. Blood pumped through Emmaline's veins with such ferocity that she could barely breathe.

As she entered the dining area, she saw Honor in the corner, overseeing his waiters as they served the guests, Elias stalking toward him with purposeful intent. Even from the distance between them, she could see the look of surprise on Honor's face as Elias approached.

Oh, good heavens, not here, not before the guests. If Father hears of this...

Her eyes shifted toward the family table and noted with relief that neither Xavier nor her father were present but her blood chilled slightly as she met Walter Greene's beady-eyed gaze from across the room.

His porcine face twisted with interest and Emmeline tore her eyes away in disgust, almost sprinting toward the men.

"Where is she?" Elias hissed at Honor.

"You cannot do this in here," Emmeline told them in a low voice. "You must come with me, both of you."

Honor opened his mouth to protest but Emmeline's scathing look seemed to stop the words from leaving his mouth.

"At once," she insisted. "Come along."

She led the way out of the dining room and through the lobby toward the mezzanine where she closed them inside a parlor for privacy.

"What is the meaning of this?" Honor choked. "I have banished you from the hotel, Mr. Compton."

"He is here as my guest," Emmeline interjected curtly. "And you will answer his questions honestly, Honor."

"I-I have nothing to say to him!" Honor sputtered, looking from Elias to Emmeline.

"Where is Christiana?" Elias hissed. "I demand to see her at once!"

"I do not—"

He was not permitted another chance to lie as Elias thrust him against the far wall, Honor gasping. Elias' forearm met Honor's windpipe.

"If you think I will leave so easily, you are mistaken," Elias growled. "I do not care what condition you have put her in, I only wish to see her with my own eyes."

"She does not wish to see you, Mr. Compton!" Honor snarled. "Or she would have contacted you by now."

"Then she may say as much to my face, Mr. Wesley. Where is she? Do not make me ask you again!"

"Honor!" Emmeline called nervously. "Please, do tell him where is his wife. He is worried about Christiana, nothing more."

"Unhand me and I will take you to her," Honor grumbled, his eyes flashing with indignation. "But I assure you, she has no interest in seeing you."

"I heard you the first time you said as much."

Emmeline watched as Honor was released, his body slumping towards the ground as he gasped to reclaim his lost breaths and Elias towered over him.

"Bring me to her."

"I will—after my shift—"

"You will do it now or you will not work again for many shifts," Elias threatened.

"I will see you covered, Honor," Emmeline told him quickly. "Please, the quicker we can see Christiana, the quicker we can confirm what you have told us."

Elias cast her a sidelong look and Emmeline realized he had heard the use of "we."

We are in this together now, she thought silently and somehow, Elias seemed to understand her sentiment.

"You should heed the lady," Elias told Honor who had finally managed to lift himself up to his full height and glower at them both.

"Very well," Honor muttered. "She is staying at a room in town until we find a house of our own."

Elias scoffed and Emmeline felt a pang of upset at the words.

"A room of *your own*? She has promised to live with you, has she?" Elias laughed but there was no mirth in his voice. "Did you know she was married?"

"You do not understand," Honor grunted. "She was trying to spare you, Mr. Compton. You have never known the whole truth about Christiana."

"Enough talk," Elias insisted. "If she chooses to stay with you, I cannot and will not stop her, but I demand to see her at once."

"As you wish. Come along."

The men shuffled toward the doorway and Emmeline stood, uncertain if she should join them or remain. Elias paused and glanced at her.

"Are you not coming?" he asked and she caught the hint of pleading in his voice.

He wishes me to accompany him, she realized with both relief and dismay. Emmeline was not sure she would be able to hold her tongue when confronted with a woman who treated Elias so horribly.

She has not only ruined his life, trapping him into a marriage, but she also mocks him with her endless affairs. Still, he worries after her.

"Of course I will come," Emmeline breathed, gathering her skirts and following the men.

If I cannot hold my tongue, surely she will be deserving of every word. Someone ought to tell her how selfish and cruel she has been to Elias over the years. Even if it cannot change matters of the present, perhaps she will show a modicum of decency in the future.

Yet, Emmeline did not have high hopes for the future, not for Elias and not for herself, not when it pertained to matters of the heart.

————

The landlady gave the trio a wary looking over when they appeared on the steps of the boarding house.

"Mr. Wesley," she said coldly. "You brought others."

"Yes, Mrs. Hammersmith. Permit me to introduce Miss Emmeline Balfour and her man."

Mrs. Hammersmith's eyes widened in recognition.

"Of course," she cooed, her tone changing instantly. "You are Mr. Balfour's lovely daughter. Welcome, and I understand congratulations are in order on your recent betrothal."

My word, terrible news does travel fast, Emmeline thought grimly but she managed a courteous smile.

"Thank you, Mrs. Hammersmith. Where might I find Miss Compton's room?"

The landlady looked perplexed. She whipped her head around to look at Honor who purposely avoided her gaze.

"Miss Compton?" she echoed. "I thought you—"

"I will see them to her," Honor interjected smoothly, leading the way toward the narrow staircase. "This way."

"Her *man?*" Elias muttered, his mind still stuck on the crass introduction. "Do I look like a servant?"

"You tried to pass as one not three days ago," Honor reminded him smugly.

"What was the meaning of Mrs. Hammersmith's confusion?" Emmeline asked, ignoring their squabbling. "Has Christiana been using an alias while here?"

"You may ask her all you want yourselves," Honor muttered, stopping before a door atop the staircase. He knocked firmly.

"Christa, it is me," he called softly. "Do not be alarmed, but I have others with me."

There was no answer before he opened the door and Emmeline stared into the dimly lit room. There was not even a small window to let in the graying winter light—only a single candle illuminated the tiny space.

Inside, Christiana sat wrapped in a quilt wearing only her bedclothes, her hair dishevelled as she stared blankly at them in surprise.

"Eli!" she choked. "W-what are you doing here?"

Elias stalked forward, his face contorted in anger, and stopped at the edge of her bed.

"Could you not have sent word at the very least?" he snapped, his face crimson. "I have been at my wits' end with worry over your whereabouts!"

"Forgive me," she mumbled, looking down at the worn quilt in which she was wrapped. "I had hoped you would move on without me."

"Oh Christa!" he yelled. "What have you entangled yourself in this time?"

"You shall not speak to her in such a manner!" Honor barked. "She has endured far enough."

"I have been through every one of her endurances alongside her!" Elias growled back. "Much to my own detriment, I might add. Moreover, I am her husband and will speak to her in any manner I please. Goodness knows she deserves much more than a chiding."

It was then that Christiana recognized that Emmeline was also in the room. "No, no," Christiana moaned. "Has your father sent you?" she whispered. "I swear, I will tell no one who the true sire of the child is. Honor and I will leave and you will never see us again."

As her words sunk in, Emmeline was rocked with devastation. She realized that Antoinette had spoken the truth.

"It is true then?" Elias asked. "You are with child?"

"I will raise him as my own!" Honor cried, stepping forward. "I will make up for all the wrongs I have committed in the past."

"Who is the father of the baby, Christa?" Elias demanded but Emmeline already knew.

"Walter Greene." Emmaline croaked. "He is the father, is he not?"

Christiana nodded, keeping her eyes carefully fixed on her trembling hands.

"I promised your father I would take the money he gave me to leave town but...I...uh...I wanted to see Walter myself. I could not believe he would simply send me away. The night I went to meet him, I sent word that I would wait for him by the River Thames but it was Honor who came, not Walter. I thought he had come to kill me."

"You should be grateful he sent me and not a true killer," Honor told Christiana. "If Walter learns that Christa is still here in Luton and that I did not do what I had been ordered to do..."

"Why did you not write me? Why did you not come home?" Elias was as conflicted by the story as Emmeline. Without waiting for an answer from Christiana, he turned to question Honor. "Why did you not kill her?"

Christiana raised her head and shared a look with Honor before turning her attention toward Elias.

"I came to Luton for a reason, Eli," she told him quietly. "I came because of Honor."

Emmeline glanced at Elias, but the tale was only growing more complicated by the moment.

"I do not understand," he replied. "You knew Honor already?"

Christiana inhaled shakily and nodded.

"He was the father of the child I lost."

Elias reeled backward as if he had been physically struck.

"You have known where he was all along? You claimed he left town for another woman."

"I did leave town," Honor replied. "But I never lived in Peterborough. I was raised at the Balfour Hotel and that is where I was employed. I had a woman here, and then I met Christiana."

"Susanna," Emmeline murmured. "You were courting Susanna."

Honor nodded and sighed, his head lowered.

"I was courting Susanna, a chambermaid at the hotel when I met Christiana."

"You impregnated Christa! Did you know?" Elias demanded, looking about in bewilderment from Honor to Christiana. "Did you ever tell him?"

"I did not," Christiana confessed, tears welling in her eyes. "I thought he loved her. I thought that despite what we had done, his heart still belonged to her and that he wanted to go home to her. I could not bring myself to tell him I was with child and force him to stay."

"It was his duty to stay!" Elias roared and Emmeline's heart swelled with pity for Elias, the man whose kindness and sense of honor had trapped him in the middle of such a mess. "*He* should have married you, not me! You knew all along that he was responsible—"

Elias abruptly stopped speaking as if there was no more air left in his lungs and Emmeline reached a hand out to touch his arm comfortingly, ignoring Honor's shocked expression as he watched the unsolicited gesture.

He has no right to judge me, not after what he has done, Emmeline thought, willing Elias to look at her. Their eyes met and she could feel the rage and grief emanating from him.

"Elias, you must listen to me," Christiana said urgently. "There is more than you understand."

"I understand," Elias spat. "I understand that you have always done what is best for yourself with little to no regard for anyone else..."

He paused before turning back to face Honor.

"How did she become pregnant with Walter Greene's child if the two of you had planned to be together?"

Instantly, Honor and Christiana looked away, their faces an identical shade of scarlet. Emmeline waited but Elias seemed to understand, possibly suspecting the worst of his wife already.

"You seduced him," Elias intoned dully. "Purposely. Hoping for financial gain."

"No!" Emmeline gasped but the expression on both their faces told her that what Elias spoke was the truth.

"Elias, I did it to protect you," Christiana murmured. "You do not understand. The money was to provide me an escape so that you could finally move forward with your life. Once I was fit to travel and had left Luton, I was going to write you and explain everything—"

"How am I to move forth with my life when you are in the wind, Christa? While you disappear and indulge your whims, I would still be the foolish man who married you without recourse," Elias scoffed, shaking his head. His parlor was white and Emmeline felt nauseous for him.

"No," Honor told him. "You are not."

"I am not what?" Elias growled. "You are a bigger fool than I if you think she will not soon tire of you and render the same treatment upon you. Fortunately for you, you are not bound to her by marriage."

"Nor are you, Elias," Christiana replied softly. She nodded toward Honor.

"What nonsense are you going on about now?" he demanded. "Of course I am or have you forgotten how I tried to protect you when you came to me in hysterics?"

"I have forgotten nothing about the kindness you have shown me," Christiana replied and Honor dropped to his knees, reaching beneath the brass bedframe to pull out a trunk.

"I wish I could have been the wife you deserved, Eli. You are a good, decent man who has always looked after me, even when I did not deserve it. You have sacrificed so much for me."

"A lot of gratitude you have shown, Christa," Elias grunted but his eyes, like Emmeline's were on Honor who rose from the floor, a paper in his hand.

"Look at this," Honor told Elias, lowering his head shamefully. "But do try to keep your wits about you."

Elias took it and Emmeline stepped closer to read what was written on the page.

"I do not..."

"Oh my..." Emmeline gasped. "I-is this a true document from the church?"

"The date..." Elias breathed. "It is three months before our wedding, Christa."

"Yes," Christiana conceded. "Do you understand what this means, Eli?"

His head swiveled to look at her in disgust.

"We were never married. You married Mr. Wesley three months before me."

CHAPTER TWELVE

Four Weeks Later

"You look lovely, my dear," Xavier told her, a smile plastered on his face. "I daresay, I have never seen a more radiant bride in all my days."

"Is that a fact?" Emmeline asked sweetly. "I do hope this is a day to recall for years to come."

"I am certain it will be the talk of Luton for many moons," Xavier said, patting her arm and meeting her gaze in the mirror. "I will tend to Mother and return to meet you in the lobby. The guests are gathered to see you in your bridal glory."

"And my fiancé?" she asked. Xavier's smile faltered.

"He is there too."

"Brilliant."

Xavier paused to study her face carefully, concern laced with suspicion creased his brow.

"I must confess, Emmy, I am rather surprised at this about face you have done regarding this marriage."

"There is no point in fighting the inevitable, is there?" Emmeline replied mysteriously, but her brother did not seem to hear the under-lying message in her words.

"I did mean what I said to you," he told her earnestly. "I will always protect you. You must know that."

"I know you are a good brother," she conceded. "But you must not worry about me, Xavy. I am confident in my future for the first time in a long while."

He gave her a lopsided grin.

"You remain my cockeyed optimist," he told her, placing a delicate kiss upon her cheek. "I will return to see you to the staircase. Father must be antsy by now. You know how he loathes to wait."

He is not the only one, Emmeline thought grimly. She turned back toward the glass, examining her blue lace gown. Her brother had not been fibbing; she looked radiant in the frilly garment.

Carefully, she adjusted the veil over her face and stepped out of the bedchambers and into the sitting room. She had asked that she not be escorted by a horde of ladies for the event and her mother, in a drunken stupor, had agreed.

There was a knock at the door and Emmeline's eyes shifted toward the clock.

Impeccable timing, she thought happily.

"You may enter."

As her father stepped across the threshold, out in the hall she noticed Joshua standing with his eyes cast downward.

"Are you quite ready, darling? The guests are growing restless."

"I am," she replied, looping her arm through his as they stepped out of her suite.

A rush of heat tinged her cheeks and a burst of anxiety fluttered in her gut.

Dear God in Heaven, please see us all through this. Amen.

They made their way to the top landing and Emmeline gasped at the sight of the guests below. She had seen fewer at royal weddings and guilt began to eat at her.

Then, she noticed her betrothed near the entranceway but Walter barely looked up at her as he shifted uncomfortably from one foot to the other.

In a strange way, Emmeline knew she was doing him a favor, despite the way it was being done. She wasn't sure how she felt about that. Did he deserve any favors?

"Come along," Charlton muttered. Emmeline had not realized she had paused and she accepted her father's gentle tug as they descended the stairs.

As she neared the bottom, she found her breaths becoming raggedy and for a terrifying moment, she was afraid she might faint dead away.

You will not swoon. You will hold your head high and finish this as we have planned for a month.

In her mind's eye, the past weeks slid by in a series of images. She could see the grateful look in Christiana's eyes when Emmeline had given her money enough to leave for Cambridge and start anew with Honor. She recalled the regret on Elias' face when he boarded the coach to return to Peterborough.

In her mind, she heard the echo of his promises to her and her heart quickened.

"Emmy," her father muttered, and again she saw she had drifted off elsewhere, nearly tripping over the clergy who had been sent by the church to marry them.

"Forgive me, Father," she said to the priest who nodded curtly.

She shifted her body toward Walter Greene who grunted inappropriately and she waited for him to lift her veil which he did not do until Xavier whispered for him to do so.

With thick, clumsy fingers, he carelessly brushed the heavy lace cover from her face and stared at her with cold, hard eyes.

"Shall we begin?" the priest asked.

Emmeline said nothing but as she tried to avoid Walter Greene's gaze, she was filled with a peculiar feeling of both pity and contempt for the man with whom she had been matched.

"Let us get this over with," he snapped and inexplicably, Emmeline found his words amusing.

"My sentiments precisely," she informed him. His mouth dropped in surprise and Emmeline did not need to look at her father's disapproving gaze to feel it radiating from him.

"Before we commence," Emmeline said. "I have something I would like to say."

There was a murmur of confusion in the crowd.

"Emmeline," Charlton hissed. "This is highly unusual."

"I agree, Father. Everything about this is unusual. For example, how is it you have come to be so indebted to Mr. Greene?"

The mutterings grew louder and this time she did look at her father, his shock almost palpable.

"Emmeline!"

"Yes, Father?"

"How dare you!"

"I dare because I believe I am deserving to know why I have been auctioned off to this man who, as all of Luton knows, is nothing more than a bookmaker. You have gotten indebted to a ruffian and a scoundrel and I am your way out of it, am I not?"

The crowd was intrigued and awed by Emmeline's questions but Charlton was incensed. He grabbed his daughter by the arm and yanked her toward his office.

"Pardon us, Father," he hissed. "We will return in one moment's time."

As she had expected, Emmeline was shoved unceremoniously inside the office and she waited for Charlton to unleash his fury upon her.

"What is the meaning of this?" he choked, his face purple with rage. "You wish to humiliate me before the entire town?"

"Not you, Father but Mr. Greene," Emmeline replied evenly. "Not that I am telling them anything they do not know about him. It is hardly a secret that you have aligned yourself with a criminal, Father."

"Do you not realize how your behavior affects the hotel?" Charlton hissed, his breaths short and wheezy.

"And what of bringing a bookmaker into the hotel as an owner?" Emmeline countered. "How does that look for the hotel? We cater to royalty, Father, noblemen and aristocrats. What were you thinking?"

Charlton's looked as though he was about to burst.

"I do not have a choice," he thundered. "If I do not pay him what is owed, I have no idea what he will do."

"Father," Emmeline told him gently. "He has no interest in marrying me. He only wishes to take a stake in this hotel. We will find another way to get him the money he is owed, but I assure you, if you allow him a stake in our legacy, it will be the beginning of the end for the Balfours."

"You speak as though you have another idea in mind," Charlton said bitterly. "We have not the money to repay our debts, not in full and that is what he demands."

"I have found a way, Father, but I will need to marry another to do so and I insist you give him the same offer you gave Mr. Greene. Thirty percent of the hotel."

"Why would I agree to sell to a stranger?" Charlton demanded, aghast. "For all I know, he will be just as unfair a business partner!"

It did not escape Emmeline's notice that he did not much care who she married provided his precious hotel was secure.

It should not hurt that I am but a commodity to be bartered or sold, but it does.

"He is a good man, a fair man and a man who will sell his own family's business to pay off *your* debts."

Charlton gaped at her.

"You cannot be serious. Who is he?"

"Does it matter, Father? We know who he is not—Walter Greene."

Father and daughter stared at one another for a long, silent moment but it was Charlton who looked away first, shaking his head in defeat.

"If I had known you would drive such a hard deal, Emmy, I would have made you my heir and not Xavier."

He was jesting, of course, but it was the first time in her life that Emmeline had ever felt she had gained an iota of respect from her father.

"Is it a deal, then, Father?"

"I suppose it is...however, someone must tell Mr. Greene."

Emmeline beamed happily and nodded.

"That would be my pleasure to arrange," she told him earnestly.

"He will not take it well, Emmeline," Charlton warned her.

"He will when I divulge that Christiana and his child are still very much alive, Father."

She did not permit him a response as she glided out of the office toward the front of the lobby where she had left Walter Greene.

———

The guests began to disperse, some lingering about as if they longed to hear a snippet of last-minute gossip before returning to their respective households, but as they filtered away, a coach and six appeared.

Emmeline's heart skipped wildly and she ran down the front steps to greet the gleaming black carriage.

The coachman barely had time to open the door before Elias hopped out, blinking against the blinding winter sunshine. His dazzling smile rivaled the sun as he gazed down at her.

"You came!" she breathed happily, studying him from barely a pace away.

"Did you have any doubt?" he asked and she shook her head vehemently, her blonde curls bobbing.

"I have no doubts about you whatsoever."

Oblivious to the stares of the remaining guests, Emmeline threw herself into Elias' arms and embraced him tightly. He held fast to her and they remained pressed against one another for a long moment, not caring who gaped openly at the display.

"You are unscathed," he murmured. "I was concerned it would not go as planned and I would come here to find you a married woman."

"Ah," she tittered. "It sounds as though it is you who was plagued with doubts."

Elias stepped back and cupped her chin in his hand, shaking his head.

"I have never been surer of anything than I am of you," he promised her. "From the moment I first saw you, I felt grounded, confident."

"Come inside," she urged, linking her arm through his. "I will show you your office."

Elias chuckled.

"How did your father handle the news?"

"Better than I expected," she replied honestly. "Confidentially, I believe he was relieved that he was given an escape."

"And Mr. Greene?"

"After I explained the situation to him, he disappeared quite abruptly. Joshua told me he left word to have his items transported to London."

Elias stopped walking and peered at her.

"Do you believe that Mr. Wesley and Christa are safe?" he asked quietly and Emmeline was touched by his concern.

"I have been in communication with Honor and he assures me they are doing well. He is consumed with regret, although I am sure that is small consolation to you after all you have endured."

"I do not wish for him to be woeful for what has happened," Elias replied quickly. "I only wish to put the past behind us and to start anew."

Emmeline agreed, patting his arm gently. "You are a good man, Elias. I am glad I will be your wife."

"My first wife."

"Your only wife!" she exclaimed, and they laughed as they entered the hotel lobby.

"Elias!" Joshua cried when his eyes fell on the older man. "You have returned!"

"Indeed," Elias replied and Joshua blushed, lowering his eyes.

"Forgive me. Mr. Compton."

"I think it is fair to call us friends, Josh," Elias told him quietly. "You may always call me Elias when we are alone."

"I-I will try not to confuse the issue," Joshua muttered, looking nervously at Emmeline.

"If you call him Elias, you best call me Emmeline too," she insisted, a slight exasperation to her tone. "I will be appalled if you do not. I did throw you in the mud more times than Elias."

Joshua giggled and nodded.

"I will try, Miss—uh, Emmeline." He looked about as though he expected God to strike him down for such a blunder and shuffled away, his ears pink.

"There will be a lot of changes upcoming," Elias commented. "I do hope everyone will conform."

"I assure you they will," Emmeline said. "The Balfour Hotel has been here a long while and we did not survive without change."

Their eyes locked and they shared a private smile.

"I have never run a hotel before," Elias confessed. "Will it be difficult?"

Emmeline laughed and tugged on his arm.

"It is not the hotel which should worry you," she told him softly. "It is the Balfours themselves."

EPILOGUE

The rose gardens were in full bloom and the heady scent was causing Emmeline's gut to flip.

"Are you well, Emmy? You look the color of fresh milk."

She tried to smile to reassure her mother, but the expression escaped in a quiver.

"I believe I should lie down for a while," she said, rising from the wicker chair and fanning herself as a rush of heat stained her face.

Anne snapped her fingers and Cora appeared.

"Cora, see Mrs. Compton to her room and send for the surgeon."

"There is no need for a doctor, Mother," Emmeline muttered, but the words were hard to say against the bile forming in her throat. Quickly, she clamped her mouth closed and swallowed, warding off the sickness which threatened to consume her.

"Oh, I daresay there is," Anne replied slyly, reaching for her glass of port. Her eyes were bloodshot and bleary but held a glimmering of knowledge. Emmeline did not bother to question her and instead stumbled out of the lush garden toward the back entrance of the hotel.

"There is no need to call Dr. Forrester," Emmeline told Cora as they made their way up the stairs slowly.

Why must the family take the fifth floor? She bemoaned silently but it had never troubled her until that moment.

"Shall I call on the waiters to carry you up?" Cora asked with concern. Emmeline's face flushed with embarrassment.

"Certainly not!" She could not fathom a more humiliating idea.

"Mrs. Compton, you are white as a sheet," Cora whispered. "Please, remain on the landing. I will call for you husband."

Cora hurried away and Emmeline scowled.

I must have eaten something disagreeable, she reasoned, but she did not move lest her wobbly legs fail. In seconds, it seemed, Elias appeared by her side, his face stricken with concern.

"My word! What is it?" he demanded, sweeping her up in his arms. "Are you ill?"

"I am merely faint. It must be the heat," Emmeline fibbed. "There is no need for such a fuss!"

Elias turned to Cora.

"Send for Dr. Forrester at once!" he barked, striding up the stairs as if she weighed no more than a feather.

"Eli," Emmeline protested. "I assure you—"

"You assure me nothing," he interrupted. "The surgeon will look you over and that is the end of the discussion."

She knew it was futile to protest and in her heart, she rather relished the comfort of being wrapped in her husband's strong arms.

He lay her on the bed of their shared chamber, propping pillows behind her head before securing a wet compress for her.

No sooner had he started to dab at her face did a knock come at the door.

"Enter," he called and Dr. Forrester appeared with his bag, a frown darkening his wrinkled face.

"What have we here?" he asked, hurrying toward them.

"I am certain it merely a case of disagreeable food," Emmeline sighed but the surgeon would hear nothing of it and he dismissed Elias from the room.

"Some privacy, Mr. Compton. I have some rather delicate questions for your wife."

"I will be in the salon," he promised her and Emmeline nodded, smiling.

"I assure you, this is nothing."

"We shall see," Dr. Forrester intoned, closing the sliding doors on Elias' face. "Now, describe your symptoms."

"I am merely a bit nauseous," she replied. "Perhaps a bit faint."

"I see. Have you any tenderness anywhere?"

The question puzzled Emmeline.

"Tenderness?"

The doctor gestured to his chest and she widened her eyes.

"Indeed!" she gasped. "How did you know?"

A slow smile formed on his lips.

"I wager that you have little to worry about, Mrs. Compton. The sickness will pass as your womb grows."

It took several seconds for her to process his words and when she did, she could only gape at the surgeon in disbelief.

"M-my womb?" she repeated. "I-I am with child?"

Without warning, the doors slid apart and Elias sprinted inside, his face alight with joy.

"A baby? We are blessed with a baby?" he choked. The doctor cast him a reproving look.

"This was a private interview, Mr. Compton," Dr. Forrester scolded but Elias did not seem to hear him as he lunged toward his wife, embracing her in his arms.

"A baby," he whispered, his eyes glowing.

"Our baby," Emmeline giggled as he slid his hand over her stomach. Gently, Elias placed a kiss on her forehead and Emmeline buried her head into his shoulder, exhaling in relief.

"Much better news than bad food," Dr. Forrester quipped and the Comptons chuckled.

"I will check back with you in a day or two," the physician told Emmeline. "If you are experiencing sickness now, I would wager you are two months along or so."

"Thank you, Doctor," Emmeline called but her gaze was still locked on Elias. Neither noticed when the older man left, the happiness overwhelming them.

"Did you hear that?" Elias murmured. "Come the new year, we will have our first child."

"Yes," Emmeline breathed. "The youngest heir to the Balfour Hotel."

————

Next book: The Hotelier's Bride

I'd like to thank you for reading this book. I hope you enjoyed it.

Please view my other titles at:
https://books2read.com/amandadavis

Printed in Great Britain
by Amazon

41414000R00067